Samuel French Acting Edition

Top Girls
A Play

by Caryl Churchill

SAMUELFRENCH.COM   SAMUELFRENCH.CO.UK

FOR PRODUCTION ENQUIRIES

UNITED STATES AND CANADA
Info@SamuelFrench.com
1-866-598-8449

UNITED KINGDOM AND EUROPE
Plays@SamuelFrench.co.uk
020-7255-4302

Each title is subject to availability from Samuel French, depending upon country of performance. Please be aware that *TOP GIRLS* may not be licensed by Samuel French in your territory. Professional and amateur producers should contact the nearest Samuel French office or licensing partner to verify availability.

The author gratefully acknowledges use of the following books:

The Confessions of Lady Nijo, translated from the Japanese by Karen Brazell, and published by Peter Owen Ltd., London

A Curious Life for a Lady (about Isabella Bird) by Pat Barr, originally published by Macmillan, London

TOP GIRLS was first produced at the
Royal Court in August 1982

PUBLIC/NEWMAN

A NEW YORK SHAKESPEARE FESTIVAL PRODUCTION

JOSEPH PAPP
PRESENTS
THE ROYAL COURT THEATRE PRODUCTION OF

TOP GIRLS

BY
Caryl Churchill

DIRECTED BY
Max Stafford-Clark

(British cast)

SCENERY BY
Peter Hartwell

COSTUMES BY
Pam Tait

LIGHTING BY
Robin Myerscough-Walker

WITH

Selina Cadell   Lindsay Duncan   Deborah Findlay   Carole Hayman
Lesley Manville   Gwen Taylor   Lou Wakefield

THE CAST
(in order of appearance)

Marlene . . . . GWEN TAYLOR

Waitress/Kit/Shona . . . . LOU WAKEFIELD

Isabella Bird/Joyce/Mrs. Kidd . . . . DEBORAH FINDLAY

Lady Nijo/Win . . . . LINDSAY DUCAN

Dull Gret/Angie . . . . CAROLE HAYMAN

Pope Joan/Louise . . . . SELINA CADELL

Patient Griselda/Nell/Jeanine . . . . LESLEY MANVILLE

ACT I

Scene 1   A Restaurant

Scene 2   'Top Girls' Employment Agency, London

Scene 3   Joyce's backyard in Suffolk

THERE WILL BE ONE FIFTEEN-MINUTE INTERMISSION.

ACT II

Scene 1   'Top Girls' Employment Agency

Scene 2   A Year Earlier. Joyce's kitchen

Production Supervisor for the New York Shakespeare Festival:
JASON STEVEN COHEN

5

PUBLIC/NEWMAN

JOSEPH PAPP

PRESENTS

THE NEW YORK SHAKESPEARE FESTIVAL COMPANY

IN

THE ROYAL COURT THEATRE PRODUCTION OF

TOP GIRLS

BY
Caryl Churchill

DIRECTED BY
Max Stafford-Clark   (American cast)

SCENERY BY
Peter Hartwell

COSTUMES BY
Pam Tait

LIGHTING BY
Robin Myerscough-Walker

WITH

**Sara Botsford   Donna Bullock   Kathryn Grody   Lise Hilboldt
Linda Hunt   Valerie Mahaffey   Freda Foh Shen**

THE CAST
(in order of appearance)

Marlene .... LISE HILBOLDT

Waitress/Jeanine/Win .... DONNA BULLOCK

Isabella Bird/Joyce/Nell .... SARA BOTSFORD

Lady Nijo/Mrs. Kidd .... FREDA FOH SHEN

Dull Gret/Angie .... KATHRYN GRODY

Pope Joan/Louise .... LINDA HUNT

Patient Griselda/Kit/Shona .... VALERIE MAHAFFEY

UNDERSTUDIES: For Dull Gret/Angie/Pope Joan/Louise—**Elaine Hausman;** For Patient Griselda/Kit/Shona/Waitress/Jeanine/Win—**Sherie Berk;** For Marlene/Lady Nijo/Mrs. Kidd—**Fredi Olster;** For Isabella Bird/Joyce/Nell— **Dale Hodges.**

ACT I

Scene 1 A restaurant

Scene 2 'Top Girls' Employment Agency, London

Scene 3 Joyce's backyard in Suffolk

THERE WILL BE ONE FIFTEEN-MINUTE INTERMISSION.

ACT II

Scene 1 'Top Girls' Employment Agency

Scene 2 A year earlier. Joyce's kitchen

Production Supervisor for the New York Shakespeare Festival: **JASON STEVEN COHEN**

PRODUCTION NOTE

The seating order for ACT I Scene 1 in the original production at the Royal Court was (from r.) Gret, Nijo, Marlene, Joan, Griselda, Isabella.

The Characters
ISABELLA BIRD (1831–1904)—lived in Edinburgh, travelled extensively between the ages of 40 and 70.
LADY NIJO (b. 1258)—Japanese, was an Emperor's courtesan and later a Buddhist nun who travelled on foot through Japan.
DULL GRET—is the subject of the Brueghel painting *Dulle Griet,* in which a woman in an apron and armour leads a crowd of women charging through hell and fighting the devils.
POPE JOAN—disguised as a man, is thought to have been Pope between 854–856.
PATIENT GRISELDA—is the obedient wife whose story is told by Chaucer in "The Clerk's Tale" of *The Canterbury Tales.*

The Layout
A speech usually follows the one immediately before it BUT:

1) When one character starts speaking before the other has finished, the point of interruption is marked /. e.g.
    ISABELLA. This is the Emperor of Japan? / I once met the Emperor of Morocco.
    NIJO. In fact he was the ex-Emperor.

2) A character sometimes continues speaking right through another's speech: e.g.
    ISABELLA. When I was forty I thought my life was over. / Oh I was pitiful. I was

NIJO. I didn't say I felt it for twenty years. Not every minute.

ISABELLA. sent on a cruise for my health and felt even worse. Pains in my bones, pins and needles . . . etc.

3) Sometimes a speech follows on from a speech earlier than the one immediately before it, and continuity is marked *. e.g.

GRISELDA. I'd seen him riding by, we all had. And he'd seen me in the fields with the sheep.*

ISABELLA. I would have been well suited to minding sheep.

NIJO. And Mr Nugent went riding by.

ISABELLA. Of course not, Nijo, I mean a healthy life in the open air.

JOAN. *He just rode up while you were minding the sheep and asked you to marry him?

where "in the fields with the sheep" is the cue to both "I would have been" and "He just rode up".

Top Girls

ACT ONE

SCENE 1

Restaurant. Saturday night. There is a table with a white cloth set for dinner with six places. The lights come up on MARLENE and the Waitress.

MARLENE. Excellent, yes, table for six. One of them's going to be late but we won't wait. I'd like a bottle of Frascati straight away if you've got one really cold. (*The Waitress goes. ISABELLA BIRD arrives.*) Here we are. Isabella.

ISABELLA. Congratulations, my dear.

MARLENE. Well, it's a step. It makes for a party. I haven't time for a holiday. I'd like to go somewhere exotic like you but I can't get away. I don't know how you could bear to leave Hawaii. / I'd like to lie

ISABELLA. I did think of settling.

MARLENE. in the sun forever, except of course I can't bear sitting still.

ISABELLA. I sent for my sister Hennie to come and join me. I said, Hennie we'll live here forever and help the natives. You can buy two sirloins of beef for what a pound of chops cost in Edinburgh. And Hennie wrote back, the dear, that yes, she would come to Hawaii if I wished, but I said she had far better stay where she was. Hennie was suited to life in Tobermory.

MARLENE. Poor Hennie.

ISABELLA. Do you have a sister?

MARLENE. Yes in fact.

ISABELLA. Hennie was happy. She was good. I did miss its face, my own pet. But I couldn't stay in Scotland. I loathed the constant murk.

11

(*LADY NIJO arrives.*)

MARLENE. (*seeing her*) Ah! Nijo! (*The Waitress enters with the wine.*)

NIJO. Marlene! (*to ISABELLA*) So excited when Marlene told me / you were coming.

ISABELLA. I'm delighted / to meet you.

MARLENE. I think a drink while we wait for the others. I think a drink anyway. What a week. (*MARLENE seats NIJO. The Waitress pours the wine.*)

NIJO. It was always the men who used to get so drunk. I'd be one of the maidens, passing the sake.

ISABELLA. I've had sake. Small hot drink. Quite fortifying after a day in the wet.

NIJO. One night my father proposed three rounds of three cups, which was normal, and then the Emperor should have said three rounds of three cups, but he said three rounds of nine cups, so you can imagine. Then the Emperor passed his sake cup to my father and said, "Let the wild goose come to me this spring."

MARLENE. Let the what?

NIJO. It's a literary allusion to a tenth-century epic, / His Majesty was very cultured.

ISABELLA. This is the Emperor of Japan? / I once met the Emperor of Morocco.

NIJO. In fact he was the ex-Emperor.

MARLENE. But he wasn't old? / Did you, Isabella?

NIJO. Twenty-nine.

ISABELLA. Oh it's a long story.

MARLENE. Twenty-nine's an excellent age.

NIJO. Well I was only fourteen and I knew he meant something but I didn't know what. He sent me an eight-layered gown and I sent it back. So when the time came

I did nothing but cry. My thin gowns were badly ripped. But even that morning when he left / —he'd a green

MARLENE. Are you saying he raped you?

NIJO. robe with a scarlet lining and very heavily embroidered trousers, I already felt different about him. It made me uneasy. No, of course not, Marlene, I belonged to him, it was what I was brought up for from a baby. I soon found I was sad if he stayed away. It was depressing day after day not knowing when he would come. I never enjoyed taking other women to him.

ISABELLA. I certainly never saw my father drunk. He was a clergyman. / And I didn't get married till I was fifty. (*The Waitress brings the menus.*)

NIJO. Oh, my father was a very religious man. Just before he died he said to me, "Serve His Majesty, be respectful, if you lose his favour enter holy orders."

MARLENE. But he meant stay in a convent, not go wandering round the country.

NIJO. Priests were often vagrants, so why not a nun? You think I shouldn't? / I still did what my father wanted.

MARLENE. No no, I think you should. / I think it was wonderful.

(*DULL GRET arrives.*)

ISABELLA. I tried to do what my father wanted.

MARLENE. Gret, good. Nijo. Gret / I know Griselda's going to be late, but should we wait for Joan? / Let's get you a drink.

ISABELLA. Hello, Gret! (*She continues to NIJO.*) I tried to be a clergyman's daughter. Needlework, music, charitable schemes. I had a tumour removed from my spine and spent a great deal of time on the sofa. I studied the metaphysical poets and hymnology. / I thought I enjoyed intellectual pursuits.

NIJO. Ah, you like poetry. I come of a line of eight generations of poets. Father had a poem / in the anthology.

ISABELLA. My father taught me Latin although I was a girl. / But really I was.

MARLENE. They didn't have Latin at my school.

ISABELLA. more suited to manual work. Cooking, washing, mending, riding horses. / Better than reading

NIJO. Oh but I'm sure you're very clever.

ISABELLA. books, eh Gret? A rough life in the open air.

NIJO. I can't say I enjoyed my rough life. What I enjoyed most was being the Emperor's favourite / and wearing thin silk.

ISABELLA. Did you have any horses, Gret?

GRET. Pig.

(*POPE JOAN arrives.*)

MARLENE. Oh Joan, thank God, we can order. Do you know everyone? We were just talking about learning Latin and being clever girls. Joan way by way of an infant prodigy. Of course you were. What excited you when you were ten?

JOAN. Because angels are without matter they are not individuals. Every angel is a species.

MARLENE. There you are. (*They laugh. They look at the menus.*)

ISABELLA. Yes, I forgot all my Latin. But my father was the mainspring of my life and when he died I was so grieved. I'll have the chicken, please, / and the soup.

NIJO. Of course you were grieved. My father was saying his prayers and he dozed off in the sun. So I touched his knee to rouse him. "I wonder what will happen," he said, and then he was dead before he finished the sentence. / If he'd

MARLENE. What a shock.

NIJO. died saying his prayers he would have gone straight to heaven. / Waldorf salad.

JOAN. Death is the return of all creatures to God.

NIJO. I shouldn't have woken him.

JOAN. Damnation only means ignorance of the truth. I was always attracted by the teachings of John the Scot, though he was inclined to confuse / God and the world.

ISABELLA. Grief always overwhelmed me at the time.

MARLENE. What I fancy is a rare steak. Gret?

ISABELLA. I am of course a member of the / Church of England.

MARLENE. Gret?

GRET. Potatoes.

MARLENE. I haven't been to church for years. / I like Christmas carols.

ISABELLA. Good works matter more than church attendance.

MARLENE. Make that two steaks and a lot of potatoes. Rare. But I don't do good works either.

JOAN. Canelloni, please, / and a salad.

ISABELLA. Well, I tried, but oh dear. Hennie did good works.

NIJO. The first half of my life was all sin and the second / all repentance.*

MARLENE. Oh what about starters?

GRET. Soup.

JOAN. *And which did you like best?

MARLENE. Were your travels just a penance? Avocado vinaigrette. Didn't you / enjoy yourself?

JOAN. Nothing to start with for me, thank you.

NIJO. Yes, but I was very unhappy. / It hurt to remember the past.

MARLENE. And the wine list.

NIJO. I think that was repentance.

MARLENE. Well I wonder.

NIJO. I might have just been homesick.

MARLENE. Or angry.

NIJO. Not angry, no, / why angry?

GRET. Can we have some more bread?

MARLENE. Don't you get angry? I get angry.

NIJO. But what about?

MARLENE. Yes let's have two more Frascati. And some more bread, please. (*The Waitress exits.*)

ISABELLA. I tried to understand Buddhism when I was in Japan but all this birth and death succeeding each other through eternities just filled me with the most profound melancholy. I do like something more active.

NIJO. You couldn't say I was inactive. I walked every day for twenty years.

ISABELLA. I don't mean walking. / I mean in the head.

NIJO. I vowed to copy five Mahayana sutras. / Do you know how long they are?

MARLENE. I don't think religious beliefs are something we have in common. Activity yes. (*GRET empties the bread basket into her apron.*)

NIJO. My head was active. / My head ached.

JOAN. It's no good being active in heresy.

ISABELLA. What heresy? She's calling the Church of England / a heresy.

JOAN. There are some very attractive / heresies.

NIJO. I had never heard of Christianity. Never / heard of it. Barbarians.

MARLENE. Well I'm not a Christian. / And I'm not a Buddhist.

ISABELLA. You have heard of it?

MARLENE. We don't all have to believe the same.

ISABELLA. I knew coming to dinner with a Pope we should keep off religion.

JOAN. I always enjoy a theological argument. But I won't try to convert you, I'm not a missionary. Anway I'm a heresy myself.

ISABELLA. There are some barbaric practices in the east.

NIJO. Barbaric?

ISABELLA. Among the lower classes.

NIJO. I wouldn't know.

ISABELLA. Well theology always made my head ache.

MARLENE. Oh good, some food. (*The Waitress brings the first course, serves it during the following, then exits.*)

NIJO. How else could I have left the court if I wasn't a nun? When father died I had only His Majesty. So when I fell out of favour I had nothing. Religion is a kind of nothing / and I dedicated what was left of me to nothing.

ISABELLA. That's what I mean about Buddhism. It doesn't brace.

MARLENE. Come on, Nijo, have some wine.

NIJO. Haven't you ever felt like that? You've all felt / like that. Nothing will ever happen again. I am dead already.

ISABELLA. You thought your life was over but it wasn't.

JOAN. You wish it was over.

GRET. Sad.

MARLENE. Yes, when I first came to London I sometimes . . . and when I got back from America I did.

But only for a few hours. Not twenty years.

ISABELLA. When I was forty I thought my life was over. / Oh I was pitiful. I was sent

NIJO. I didn't say I felt it for twenty years. Not every minute.

ISABELLA. on a cruise for my health and I felt even worse. Pains in my bones, pins and needles in my hands, swelling behind the ears, and — oh, stupidity. I shook all over, indefinable terror. And Australia seemed to me a hideous country, the acacias stank like drains. / I

NIJO. You were homesick. (GRET steals a bottle of wine.)

ISABELLA. had a photograph taken for Hennie but I told her I wouldn't send it, my hair had fallen out and my clothes were crooked, I looked completely insane and suicidal.

NIJO. So did I, exactly, dressed as a nun. / I was wearing walking shoes for the first time.

ISABELLA. I longed to go home, / but home to what? Houses are so perfectly dismal.*

NIJO. I longed to go back ten years.

MARLENE. *I thought travelling cheered you both up.

ISABELLA. Oh it did / of course. It was on

NIJO. I'm not a cheerful person, Marlene. I just laugh a lot.

ISABELLA. the trip from Australia to the Sandwich Isles, I fell in love with the sea. There were rats in the cabin and ants in the food but suddenly it was like a new world. I woke up every morning happy, knowing there would be nothing to annoy me. No nervousness. No dressing.

NIJO. Don't you like getting dressed? I adored my clothes. / When I was chosen

MARLENE. You had prettier colours than Isabella.

NIJO. to give sake to His Majesty's brother, the

Emperor Kameyana, on his formal visit, I wore raw silk
pleated trousers and a seven-layered gown in shades of
red, and two outer garments, / yellow lined with green

MARLENE. Yes, all that silk must have been very—
(*The Waitress enters, clears the first course and exits.*)

JOAN. I dressed as a boy when I left home.*

NIJO. and a light green jacket. Lady Betto had a five-
layered gown in shades of green and purple.

ISABELLA. *You dressed as a boy?

MARLENE. Of course, / for safety.

JOAN. It was easy, I was only twelve. / Also women
weren't allowed in the library. We wanted to study in
Athens.

MARLENE. You ran away alone?

JOAN. No, not alone, I went with my friend. / He was

NIJO. Ah, an elopement.

JOAN. sixteen but I thought I knew more science than
he did and almost as much philosophy.

ISABELLA. Well I always travelled as a lady and I
repudiated strongly any suggestion in the press that I
was other than feminine.

MARLENE. I don't wear trousers in the office. / I
could but I don't.

ISABELLA. There was no great danger to a woman of
my age and appearance.

MARLENE. And you got away with it, Joan?

JOAN. I did then. (*The Waitress brings in the main
course.*)

MARLENE. And nobody noticed anything?

JOAN. They noticed I was a very clever boy. / And

MARLENE. I couldn't have kept pretending for so
long.

JOAN. when I shared a bed with my friend, that was
ordinary—two poor students in a lodging house. I think
I forgot I was pretending.

ISABELLA. Rocky Mountain Jim, Mr Nugent, showed me no disrespect. He found it interesting, I think, that I could make scones and also lasso cattle. Indeed he declared his love for me, which was most distressing.

NIJO. What did he say? / We always sent poems first.

MARLENE. What did you say?

ISABELLA. I urged him to give up whisky, / but he said it was too late.

MARLENE. Oh Isabella.

ISABELLA. He had lived alone in the mountains for many years.

MARLENE. But did you—? (*The Waitress goes.*)

ISABELLA. Mr Nugent was a man that any woman might love but none could marry. I came back to England.

NIJO. Did you write him a poem when you left? / Snow on the mountains. My sleeves

MARLENE. Did you never see him again?

ISABELLA. No, never.

NIJO. are wet with tears. In England no tears, no snow.

ISABELLA. Well, I say never. One morning very early in Switzerland, it was a year later, I had a vision of him as I last saw him / in his trapper's clothes with his

NIJO. A ghost!

ISABELLA. hair round his face, and that was the day, / I learnt later, he died with a

NIJO. Ah!

ISABELLA. bullet in his brain. / He just bowed to me and vanished.

MARLENE. Oh Isabella.

NIJO. When your lover dies—One of my lovers died. / The priest Ariake.

JOAN. My friend died. Have we all got dead lovers?

MARLENE. Not me, sorry.

NIJO. (*to ISABELLA*) I wasn't a nun, I was still at court, but he was a priest, and when he came to me he dedicated his whole life to hell. / He knew that when he died he would fall into one of the three lower realms. And he died, he did die.

JOAN. (*to MARLENE*) I'd quarrelled with him over the teachings of John the Scot, who held that our ignorance of God is the same as his ignorance of himself. He only knows what he creates because he creates everything he knows but he himself is above being—do you follow?

MARLENE. No, but go on.

NIJO. I couldn't bear to think / in what shape would he be reborn.*

JOAN. St Augustine maintained that the Neo-Platonic Ideas are indivisible

ISABELLA. *Buddhism is really most uncomfortable.

JOAN. from God, but I agreed with John that the created world is essences derived from Ideas which derived from God. As Denys the Areopagite said—the pseudo-Denys—first we give God a name, then deny it, / then reconcile the contradiction

NIJO. In what shape would he return?

JOAN. by looking beyond / those terms—

MARLENE. Sorry, what? Denys said what?

JOAN. Well we disagreed about it, we quarrelled. And next day he was ill, / I was so annoyed with him

NIJO. Misery in this life and worse in the next, all because of me.

JOAN. all the time I was nursing him I kept going over the arguments in my mind. Matter is not a means of knowing the essence. The source of the species is the Idea. But then I realized he'd never understand my arguments again, and that night he died. John the Scot held that the individual disintegrates / and there is no personal immortality.

ISABELLA. I wouldn't have you think I was in love with Jim Nugent. It was yearning to save him that I felt.

MARLENE. (*to JOAN*) So what did you do?

JOAN. First I decided to stay a man. I was used to it. And I wanted to devote my life to learning. Do you know why I went to Rome? Italian men didn't have beards.

ISABELLA. The loves of my life were Hennie, my own pet, and my dear husband the doctor, who nursed Hennie in her last illness. I knew it would be terrible when Hennie died but I didn't know how terrible. I felt half of myself had gone. How could I go on my travels without that sweet soul waiting at home for my letters? It was Doctor Bishop's devotion to her in her last illness that made me decide to marry him. He and Hennie had the same sweet character. I had not.

NIJO. I thought His Majesty had sweet character because when he found out about Ariake he was so kind. But really it was because he no longer cared for me. One night he even sent me out to a man who had been pursuing me. / He lay awake on the other side of the screens and listened.

ISABELLA. I did wish marriage had seemed more of a step. I tried very hard to cope with the ordinary drudgery of life. I was ill again with carbuncles on the spine and nervous prostration. I ordered a tricycle, that was my idea of adventure then. And John himself fell ill, with erysipelas and anaemia. I began to love him with my whole heart but it was too late. He was a skeleton with transparent white hands. I wheeled him on various seafronts in a bathchair. And he faded and left me. There was nothing in my life. The doctors said I had gout / and my heart was much affected.

NIJO. There was nothing in my life, nothing, without the Emperor's favour. The Empress had always been my enemy, Marlene, she said I had no right to wear three-layered gowns. / But I was the adopted daughter of my grandfather the Prime Minister. I had been publicly granted permission to wear thin silk.

JOAN. There was nothing in my life except my studies. I was obsessed with pursuit of the truth. I taught at the Greek School in Rome, which St Augustine had made famous. I was poor, I worked hard, I spoke apparently brilliantly, I was still very young, I was a stranger, suddenly I was quite famous, I was everyone's favourite. Huge crowds came to hear me. The day after they made me cardinal I fell ill and lay two weeks without speaking, full of terror and regret. / But then I got up determined to

MARLENE. Yes, success is very . . .

JOAN. go on. I was seized again / with a desperate longing for the absolute.

ISABELLA. Yes, yes, to go on. I sat in Tobermory among Hennie's flowers and sewed a complete outfit in Jaeger flannel. / I was fifty-six years old.

NIJO. Out of favour but I didn't die. I left on foot, nobody saw me go. For the next twenty years I walked through Japan.

GRET. Walking is good. (*Meanwhile, the Waitress enters, pours lots of wine, then shows MARLENE the empty bottle.*)

JOAN. Pope Leo died and I was chosen. All right then. I would be Pope. I would know God. I would know everything.

ISABELLA. I determined to leave my grief behind and set off for Tibet.

MARLENE. Magnificent all of you. We need some

more wine, please, two bottles I think, Griselda isn't even here yet, and I want to drink a toast to you all. (*The Waitress exits.*)

ISABELLA. To yourself surely, / we're here to celebrate your success.

NIJO. Yes, Marlene.

JOAN. Yes, what is it exactly, Marlene?

MARLENE. Well it's not Pope but it is managing director.*

JOAN. And you find work for people.

MARLENE. Yes, an employment agency.

NIJO. *Over all the women you work with. And the men.

ISABELLA. And very well deserved too. I'm sure it's just the beginning of something extraordinary.

MARLENE. Well it's worth a party.

ISABELLA. To Marlene.*

MARLENE. And all of us.

JOAN. *Marlene.

NIJO. Marlene.

GRET. Marlene.

MARLENE. We've all come a long way. To our courage and the way we changed our lives and our extraordinary achievements. (*They laugh and drink a toast.*)

ISABELLA. Such adventures. We were crossing a mountain pass at seven thousand feet, the cook was all to pieces, the muleteers suffered fever and snow blindness. But even though my spine was agony I managed very well.*

MARLENE. Wonderful.

NIJO. *Once I was ill for four months lying alone at an inn. Nobody to offer a horse to Buddha. I had to live for myself, and I did live.

ISABELLA. Of course you did. It was far worse returning to Tobermory. I always felt dull when I was stationary. / That's why I could never stay anywhere.

NIJO. Yes, that's it exactly. New sights. The shrine by the beach, the moon shining on the sea. The goddess had vowed to save all living things. / She would even save the fishes. I was full of hope.

JOAN. I had thought the Pope would know everything. I thought God would speak to me directly. But of course he knew I was a woman.

MARLENE. But nobody else even suspected? (*The Waitress brings more wine and then exits.*)

JOAN. In the end I did take a lover again.*

ISABELLA. In the vatican?

GRET. *Keep you warm.

NIJO. *Ah, lover.

MARLENE. *Good for you.

JOAN. He was one of my chamberlains. There are such a lot of servants when you're Pope. The food's very good. And I realized I did know the truth. Because whatever the Pope says, that's true.

NIJO. What was he like, the chamberlain?*

GRET. Big cock.

ISABELLA. Oh, Gret.

MARLENE. *Did he fancy you when he thought you were a fella?

NIJO. What was he like?

JOAN. He could keep a secret.

MARLENE. So you did know everything.

JOAN. Yes, I enjoyed being Pope. I consecrated bishops and let people kiss my feet. I received the King of England when he came to submit to the church. Unfortunately there were earthquakes, and some village reported it had rained blood, and in France there was a plague of giant grasshoppers, but I don't think that can have been my fault, do you?* (*laughter*) The grasshoppers fell on the English Channel / and were washed up on shore

NIJO. I once went to sea. It was very lonely. I realized it made very little difference where I went.

JOAN. and their bodies rotted and poisoned the air and everyone in those parts died. (*laughter*)

ISABELLA. *Such superstition! I was nearly murdered in China by a howling mob. They thought the barbarians ate babies and put them under railway sleepers to make the tracks steady, and ground up their eyes to make the lenses of cameras. / So they were shouting,

MARLENE. And you had a camera!

ISABELLA. "Child-eater, child-eater." Some people tried to sell girl babies to Europeans for cameras or stew! (*laughter*)

MARLENE. So apart from the grasshoppers it was a great success.

JOAN. Yes, if it hadn't been for the baby I expect I'd have lived to an old age like Theodora of Alexandria, who lived as a monk. She was accused by a girl / who fell in love with her of being the father of her child and—

NIJO. But tell us what happened to your baby. I had some babies.

MARLENE. Didn't you think of getting rid of it?

JOAN. Wouldn't that be a worse sin than having it? / But a Pope with a child was about as bad as possible.

MARLENE. I don't know, you're the Pope.

JOAN. But I wouldn't have known how to get rid of it.

MARLENE. Other Popes had children, surely.

JOAN. They didn't give birth to them.

NIJO. Well you were a woman.

JOAN. Exactly and I shouldn't have been a woman. Women, children and lunatics can't be Pope.

MARLENE. So the only thing to do / was to get rid of it somehow.

NIJO. You had to have it adopted secretly.

JOAN. But I didn't know what was happening. I thought I was getting fatter, but then I was eating more and sitting about, the life of a Pope is quite luxurious. I don't think I'd spoken to a woman since I was twelve. The chamberlain was the one who realized.

MARLENE. And by then it was too late.

JOAN. Oh I didn't want to pay attention. It was easier to do nothing.

NIJO. But you had to plan for having it. You had to say you were ill and go away.

JOAN. That's what I should have done I suppose.

MARLENE. Did you want them to find out?

NIJO. I too was often in embarrassing situations, there's no need for a scandal. My first child was His Majesty's, which unfortunately died, but my second was Akebono's. I was seventeen. He was in love with me when I was thirteen, he was very upset when I had to go to the Emperor, it was very romantic, a lot of poems. Now His Majesty hadn't been near me for two months so he thought I was four months pregnant when I was really six, so when I reached the ninth month / I announced I was seriously ill,

JOAN. I never knew what month it was.

NIJO. and Akebono announced he had gone on a religious retreat. He held me round the waist and lifted me up as the baby was born. He cut the cord with a short sword, wrapped the baby in white and took it away. It was only a girl but I was sorry to lose it. Then I told the Emperor that the baby had miscarried because of my illness, and there you are. The danger was past.

JOAN. But, Nijo, I wasn't used to having a woman's body.

ISABELLA. So what happened?

JOAN. I didn't know of course that it was near the time. It was Rogation Day, there was always a procession. I was on the horse dressed in my robes and a cross was carried in front of me, and all the cardinals were following, and all the clergy of Rome, and a huge crowd of people. / We set off from St Peter's to go

MARLENE. Total Pope. (*GRET pours the wine and steals the bottle.*)

JOAN. to St John's. I had felt a slight pain earlier, I thought it was something I'd eaten, and then it came back, and came back more often. I thought when this is over I'll go to bed. There were still long gaps when I felt perfectly all right and I didn't want to attract attention to myself and spoil the ceremony. Then I suddenly realized what it must be. I had to last out till I could get home and hide. Then something changed, my breath started to catch, I couldn't plan things properly any more. We were in a little street that goes between St Clement's and the Colosseum, and I just had to get off the horse and sit down for a minute. Great waves of pressure were going through my body, I heard sounds like a cow lowing, they came out of my mouth. Far away I heard people screaming, "The Pope is ill, the Pope is dying." And the baby just slid out on to the road.*

MARLENE. The cardinals / won't have known where to put themselves.

NIJO. Oh dear, Joan, what a thing to do! In the street!

ISABELLA. *How embarrassing.

GRET. In a field, yah. (*They are laughing.*)

JOAN. One of the cardinals said, "The Antichrist!" and fell over in a faint. (*They all laugh.*)

MARLENE. So what did they do? They weren't best pleased.

JOAN. They took me by the feet and dragged me out of town and stoned me to death. (*They stop laughing.*)

MARLENE. Joan, how horrible.

JOAN. I don't really remember.

NIJO. And the child died too?

JOAN. Oh yes, I think so, yes. (*The Waitress enters to clear the plates. Pause. They start talking very quietly.*)

ISABELLA. (*to JOAN*) I never had any children. I was very fond of horses.

NIJO. (*to MARLENE*) I saw my daughter once. She was three years old. She wore a plum-red / small sleeved gown. Akebono's wife

ISABELLA. Birdie was my favourite. A little Indian bay mare I rode in the Rocky Mountains.

NIJO. had taken the child because her own died. Everyone thought I was just a visitor. She was being brought up carefully so she could be sent to the palace like I was. (*GRET steals her empty plate.*)

ISABELLA. Legs of iron and always cheerful, and such a pretty face. If a stranger led her she reared up like a bronco.

NIJO. I never saw my third child after he was born, the son of Ariake the priest. Ariake held him on his lap the day he was born and talked to him as if he could understand, and cried. My fourth child was Ariake's too. Ariake died before he was born. I didn't want to see anyone, I stayed alone in the hills. It was a boy again, my third son. But oddly enough I felt nothing for him.

MARLENE. How many children did you have, Gret?

GRET. Ten.

ISABELLA. Whenever I came back to England I felt I had so much to atone for. Hennie and John were so good. I did no good in my life. I spent years in self-gratification. So I hurled myself into committees, I nursed the people of Tobermory in the epidemic of influenza, I lectured the Young Women's Christian Association on Thrift. I talked and talked explaining how the East was corrupt and vicious. My travels must do good to someone beside myself. I wore myself out with good causes.

MARLENE. (*pause*) Oh God, why are we all so miserable?

JOAN. (*pause*) The procession never went down that street again.

MARLENE. They rerouted it specially?

JOAN. Yes they had to go all round to avoid it. And they introduced a pierced chair.

MARLENE. A pierced chair?

JOAN. Yes, a chair made out of solid marble with a hole in the seat / and it was

MARLENE. You're not serious.

JOAN. in the Chapel of the Saviour, and after he was elected the Pope had to sit in it.

MARLENE. And someone looked up his skirts? / Not really!

ISABELLA. What an extraordinary thing.

JOAN. Two of the clergy / made sure he was a man.

NIJO. On their hands and knees!

MARLENE. A pierced chair!

GRET. Balls!

(*GRISELDA arrives unnoticed.*)

NIJO. Why couldn't he just pull up his robe?

JOAN. He had to sit there and look dignified.

MARLENE. You could have made all your chamberlains sit in it.*

GRET. Big one. Small one.

NIJO. Very useful chair at court.

ISABELLA. *Or the Laird of Tobermory in his kilt.

(*They are quite drunk. They get the giggles. MARLENE notices GRISELDA and gets up to welcome her. The others go on talking and laughing. GRET crosses to JOAN and ISABELLA and pours them wine from her stolen bottles. The Waitress gives out the menus.*)

MARLENE. Griselda! / There you are. Do you want to eat?

GRISELDA. I'm sorry I'm so late. No, no, don't bother.

MARLENE. Of course it's no bother. / Have you eaten?

GRISELDA. No really, I'm not hungry.

MARLENE. Well have some pudding.

GRISELDA. I never eat pudding.

MARLENE. Griselda, I hope you're not anorexic. We're having pudding, I am, and getting nice and fat.

GRISELDA. Oh if everyone is. I don't mind.

MARLENE. Now who do you know? This is Joan who was Pope in the ninth century, and Isabella Bird, the Victorian traveller, and Lady Nijo from Japan, Emperor's concubine and Buddhist nun, thirteenth century, nearer your own time, and Gret who was painted by Brueghel. Griselda's in Boccaccio and Petrarch and Chaucer because of her extraordinary marriage I'd like profiteroles because they're disgusting.

JOAN. Zabaglione, please.

ISABELLA. Apple pie / and cream.

NIJO. What's this?

MARLENE. Zabaglione, it's Italian, it's what Joan's having, / it's delicious.

NIJO. A Roman Catholic / dessert? Yes please.

MARLENE. Gret?

GRET. Cake.

GRISELDA. Just cheese and biscuits, thank you. (*The Waitress exits.*)

MARLENE. Yes, Griselda's life is like a fairy story, except it starts with marrying the prince.

GRISELDA. He's only a marquis, Marlene.

MARLENE. Well everyone for miles around is his liege and he'd absolute lord of life and death and you were the poor but beautiful peasant girl and he whisked you off. / Near enough a prince.

NIJO. How old were you?

GRISELDA. Fifteen.

NIJO. I was brought up in court circles and it was still a shock. Had you ever seen him before?

GRISELDA. I'd seen him riding by, we all had. And he'd seen me in the fields with the sheep.*

ISABELLA. I would have been well suited to minding sheep.

NIJO. And Mr Nugent riding by.

ISABELLA. Of course not, Nijo, I mean a healthy life in the open air.

JOAN. *He just rode up while you were minding the sheep and asked you to marry him?

GRISELDA. No, no, it was on the wedding day. I was waiting outside the door to see the procession. Everyone wanted him to get married so there'd be an heir to look after us when he died, / and at last he

MARLENE. I don't think Walter wanted to get married. It is Walter? Yes.

GRISELDA. announced a day for the wedding but nobody knew who the bride was, we thought it must be a foreign princess, we were longing to see her. Then the carriage stopped outside our cottage and we couldn't see the bride anywhere. And he came and spoke to my father.

NIJO. And your father told you to serve the Prince.

GRISELDA. My father could hardly speak. The Marquis said it wasn't an order, I could say no, but if I said yes I must always obey him in everything.

MARLENE. That's when you should have suspected.

GRISELDA. But of course a wife must obey her husband. / And of course I must obey the Marquis.*

ISABELLA. I swore to obey dear John, of course, but it didn't seem to arise. Naturally I wouldn't have wanted to go abroad while I was married.

MARLENE. *Then why bother to mention it at all? He'd got a thing about it, that's why.

GRISELDA. I'd rather obey the Marquis than a boy from the village.

MARLENE. Yes, that's a point.

JOAN. I never obeyed anyone. They all obeyed me.

NIJO. And what did you wear? He didn't make you get married in your own clothes? That would be perverse.*

MARLENE. Oh, you wait.

GRISELDA. *He had ladies with him who undressed me and they had a white silk dress and jewels for my hair.

MARLENE. And at first he seemed perfectly normal?

GRISELDA. Marlene, you're always so critical of him. / Of course he was normal, he was very kind.

MARLENE. But, Griselda, come on, he took your baby.

GRISELDA. Walter found it hard to believe I loved him. He couldn't believe I would always obey him. He had to prove it.

MARLENE. I don't think Walter likes women.

GRISELDA. I'm sure he loved me, Marlene, all the time.

MARLENE. He just had a funny way / of showing it.

GRISELDA. It was hard for him too.

JOAN. How do you mean he took away your baby?

NIJO. Was it a boy?

GRISELDA. No, the first one was a girl.

NIJO. Even so it's hard when they take it away. Did you see it at all?

GRISELDA. Oh yes, she was six weeks old.

NIJO. Much better to do it straight away.

ISABELLA. But why did your husband take the child?

GRISELDA. He said all the people hated me because I was just one of them. And now I had a child they were restless. So he had to get rid of the child to keep them quiet. But he said he wouldn't snatch her, I had to agree and obey and give her up. So when I was feeding her a man came in and took her away. I thought he was going to kill her even before he was out of the room.

MARLENE. But you let him take her? You didn't struggle?

GRISELDA. I asked him to give her back so I could kiss he. And I asked him to bury her where no animals could dig her up. / It was Walter's child to do what he

ISABELLA. Oh, my dear.

GRISELDA. liked with.*

MARLENE. Walter was bonkers.

GRET. Bastard.

ISABELLA. *But surely, murder.

GRISELDA. I had promised.

MARLENE. I can't stand this. I'm going for a pee.

(*MARLENE goes out. The Waitress brings the dessert, serves it during the following, then exits.*)

NIJO. No, I understand. Of course you had to, he was your life. And were you in favour after that?

GRISELDA. Oh yes, we were very happy together. We never spoke about what had happened.

ISABELLA. I can see you were doing what you thought was your duty. But didn't it make you ill?

GRISELDA. No, I was very well, thank you.

NIJO. And you had another child?

GRISELDA. Not for four years, but then I did, yes, a boy.

NIJO. Ah a boy. / So it all ended happily.

GRISELDA. Yes he was pleased. I kept my son till he was two years old. A peasant's grandson. It made the people angry. Walter explained.

ISABELLA. But surely he wouldn't kill his children / just because—

GRISELDA. Oh it wasn't true. Walter would never give in to the people. He wanted to see if I loved him enough.

JOAN. He killed his children / to see if you loved him enough?

NIJO. Was it easier the second time or harder?

GRISELDA. It was always easy because I always knew I would do what he said. (*Pause. They start to eat.*)

ISABELLA. I hope you didn't have any more children.

GRISELDA. Oh no, no more. It was twelve years till he tested me again.

ISABELLA. So whatever did he do this time? / My poor John, I never loved him enough, and he would never have dreamt . . .

GRISELDA. He sent me away. He said the people wanted him to marry someone else who'd give him an heir and he'd got special permission from the Pope. So I said I'd go home to my father. I came with nothing / so I went with nothing. I took

NIJO. Better to leave if your master doesn't want you.

GRISELDA. off my clothes. He let me keep a slip so he wouldn't be shamed. And I walked home barefoot. My father came out in tears. Everyone was crying except me.

NIJO. At least your father wasn't dead. / I had nobody.

ISABELLA. Well it can be a relief to come home. I loved to see Hennie's sweet face again.

GRISELDA. Oh yes, I was perfectly content. And quite soon he sent for me again.

JOAN. I don't think I would have gone.

GRISELDA. But he told me to come. I had to obey him. He wanted me to help prepare his wedding. He was getting married to a young girl from France / and nobody except me knew how to arrange things the way he liked them.

NIJO. It's always hard taking him another woman. (*MARLENE comes back.*)

JOAN. I didn't live a woman's life. I don't understand it.

GRISELDA. The girl was sixteen and far more beautiful than me. I could see why he loved her. / She had her younger brother with her as a page. (*The Waitress enters.*)

MARLENE. Oh God, I can't bear it. I want some coffee. Six coffees. Six brandies. / Double brandies. Straightaway. (*The Waitress exits.*)

GRISELDA. They all went into the feast I'd prepared. And he stayed behind and put his arms round me and kissed me. / I felt half asleep with the shock.

NIJO. Oh, like a dream.

MARLENE. And he said, "This is your daughter and your son."

GRISELDA. Yes.

JOAN. What?

NIJO. Oh. Oh I see. You got them back.

ISABELLA. I did think it was remarkably barbaric to kill them but you learn not to say anything. / So he had them brought up secretly I suppose.

MARLENE. Walter's a monster. Weren't you angry?
What did you do?

GRISELDA. Well I fainted. Then I cried and kissed the
children. / Everyone was making a fuss of me.

NIJO. But did you feel anything for them?

GRISELDA. What?

NIJO. Did you feel anything for the children?

GRISELDA. Of course, I loved them.

JOAN. So you forgave him and lived with him?

GRISELDA. He suffered so much all those years.

ISABELLA. Hennie had the same sweet nature.

NIJO. So they dressed you again?

GRISELDA. Cloth of gold.

JOAN. I can't forgive anything.

MARLENE. You really are exceptional, Griselda.

NIJO. Nobody gave me back my children. (*She cries.*)

(*The Waitress brings the brandies and then exits. During
the following, JOAN goes to NIJO.*)

ISABELLA. I can never be like Hennie. I was always so
busy in England, a kind of business I detested. The very
presence of people exhausted my emotional reserves. I
could not be like Hennie however I tried. I tried and was
as ill as could be. The doctor suggested a steel net to
support my head, the weight of my own head was too
much for my diseased spine. It is dangerous to put
oneself in depressing circumstances. Why should I do
it?

JOAN. (*to NIJO*) Don't cry.

NIJO. My father and the Emperor both died in the
autumn. So much pain.

JOAN. Yes, but don't cry.

NIJO. They wouldn't let me into the palace when he
was dying. I hid in the room with his coffin, then I

couldn't find where I'd left my shoes, I ran after the
funeral procession in bare feet, I couldn't keep up.
When I got there it was over, a few wisps of smoke in
the sky, that's all that was left of him. What I want to
know is, if I'd still been at court, would I have been
allowed to wear full mourning?

MARLENE. I'm sure you would.

NIJO. Why do you say that? You don't know anything
about it. Would I have been allowed to wear full mourning?

ISABELLA. How can people live in this dim pale island
and wear our hideous clothes? I cannot and will not live
the life of a lady.

NIJO. I'll tell you something that made me angry. I
was eighteen, at the Full Moon Ceremony. They make a
special rice gruel and stir it with their sticks, and then
they beat their women across the loins so they'll have
sons and not daughters. So the Emperor beat us all /
very hard as

MARLENE. What a sod. (*The Waitress enters with the
coffees.*)

NIJO. usual—that's not it, Marlene, that's normal,
what made us angry he told his attendants they could
beat us too. Well they had a wonderful time. / So Lady
Genki and I made a plan, and the ladies

MARLENE. I'd like another brandy, please. Better
make it six. (*The Waitress exits.*)

NIJO. all hid in his rooms, and Lady Mashimizu stood
guard with a stick at the door, and when His Majesty
came in Genki seized him and I beat him till he cried out
and promised he would never order anyone to hit us
again. Afterwards there was a terrible fuss. The nobles
were horrified. "We wouldn't even dream of stepping on
Your Majesty's shadow." And I had hit him with a stick.
Yes, I hit him with a stick.

(*The Waitress brings the brandy bottle and tops up the glasses. JOAN crosses in front of the table and back to her place while drunkenly reciting:*)

JOAN. Suave, mari magno turantibus aequora ventis,
e terra magnum alterius spectare laborem;
non quia vexari quemquamst iucunda voluptas,
sed quibus ipse malis careas quia cernere suave est.
Suave etiam belli certamina magna tueri
per campos instructa tua sine parte pericli.
Sed nil dulcius est, bene quam munita tenere
edita doctrina sapientum templa serena, /
despicere unde queas alios passimque videre
errare atque viam palantis quaerere vitae,
GRISELDA. I do think—I do wonder—it would have been nicer if Walter hadn't had to.
ISABELLA. Why should I? Why should I?
MARLENE. Of course not.
NIJO. I hit him with a stick.
JOAN. certare ingenio, contendere nobilitate,
noctes atque dies niti praestante labore
ad summas emergere opes rerumque potiri.
O miseras hominum mentis, / o pectora caeca! [4]
ISABELLA. O miseras!
NIJO. *Pectora caeca!
JOAN. qualibus in tenebris vitae quantisque periclis
degitur hoc aevi quodcumquest! / none videre
nil aliud sibi naturam latrare, nisi utqui
corpore seiunctus dolor absit, mente fruatur . . . (*She subsides.*)
GRET. We come to hell through a big mouth. Hell's black and red. / It's
MARLENE. (*to JOAN*) Shut up, pet.
GRISELDA. Hush, please.
ISABELLA. Listen, she's been to hell.

GRET. like the village where I come from. There's a river and a bridge and houses. There's places on fire like when the soldiers come. There's a big devil sat on a roof with a big hole in his arse and he's scooping stuff out of it with a big ladle and it's falling down on us, and it's money, so a lot of the women stop and get some. But most of us is fighting the devils. There's lots of little devils, our size, and we get them down all right and give them a beating. There's lots of funny creatures round your feet, you don't like to look, like rats and lizards, and nasty things, a bum with a face, and fish with legs, and faces on things that don't have faces on. But they don't hurt, you just keep going. Well we'd had worse, you see, we'd had the Spanish. We'd all had family killed. My big son die on a wheel. Birds eat him. My baby, a soldier run her through with a sword. I'd had enough, I was mad, I hate the bastards. I come out of my front door that morning and shout till my neighbours come out and I said, "Come on, we're going where the evil come from and pay the bastards out." And they all come out just as they was / from baking or

NIJO. All the ladies come.

GRET. washing in their aprons, and we push down the street and the ground opens up and we go through a big mouth into a street just like ours but in hell. I've got a sword in my hand from somewhere and I fill a basket with gold cups they drink out of down there. You just keep running on and fighting, / you didn't stop for nothing. Oh we give them devils such a beating.*

NIJO. Take that, take that.

JOAN. *Something something something mortisque timores

tum vacuum pectus—damn.

Quod si ridicula—
something something on and on and on
and something splendorem purpureai.

ISABELLA. I thought I would have a last jaunt up the
west river in China. Why not? But the doctors were so
very grave I just went to Morocco. The sea was so wild I
had to be landed by ship's crane in a coal bucket. / My
horse was a terror to me, a powerful black charger.

GRET. Coal bucket good.

JOAN. nos in luce timemus
something
terrorem

(*NIJO is laughing and crying. JOAN gets up and is sick.
GRISELDA looks after her.*)

GRISELDA. Can I have some water, please? (*The Waitress exits.*)

ISABELLA. So off I went to visit the Berber sheikhs in
full blue trousers and great brass spurs. I was the only
European woman ever to have seen the Emperor of
Morocco. I was (*The Waitress brings the water.*) sev-
enty years old. What lengths to go to for a last chance of
joy. I knew my return of vigour was only temporary,
but how marvellous while it lasted.

SCENE 2

*"Top Girls" Employment Agency. Monday morning.
The Lights come up on MARLENE and JEANINE.*

MARLENE. Right, Jeanine, you are Jeanine aren't

you? Let's have a look. O's and A's. / No A's, all those

JEANINE. Six O's.

MARLENE. O's you probably could have got an A. / Speeds, not brilliant, not too bad.

JEANINE. I wanted to go to work.

MARLENE. Well, Jeanine, what's your present job like?

JEANINE. I'm a secretary.

MARLENE. Secretary or typist?

JEANINE. I did start as a typist but the last six months I've been a secretary.

MARLENE. To?

JEANINE. To three of them, really, they share me. There's Mr Ashford, he's the office manager, and Mr Philby / is sales, and—

MARLENE. Quite a small place?

JEANINE. A bit small.

MARLENE. Friendly?

JEANINE. Oh it's friendly enough.

MARLENE. Prospects?

JEANINE. I don't think so, that's the trouble. Miss Lewis is secretary to the managing director and she's been there forever, and Mrs Bradford / is—

MARLENE. So you want a job with better prospects?

JEANINE. I want a change.

MARLENE. So you'll take anything comparable?

JEANINE. No, I do want prospects. I want more money.

MARLENE. You're getting—?

JEANINE. Hundred.

MARLENE. It's not bad you know. You're what? Twenty?

JEANINE. I'm saving to get married.

MARLENE. Does that mean you don't want a long-term job, Jeanine?

JEANINE. I might do.

MARLENE. Because where do the prospects come in? No kids for a bit?

JEANINE. Oh no, not kids, not yet.

MARLENE. So you won't tell them you're getting married?

JEANINE. Had I better not?

MARLENE. It would probably help.

JEANINE. I'm not wearing a ring. We thought we wouldn't spend on a ring.

MARLENE. Saves taking it off.

JEANINE. I wouldn't take it off.

MARLENE. There's no need to mention it when you go for an interview. / Now, Jeanine, do you have a feel

JEANINE. But what if they ask?

MARLENE. for any particular kind of company?

JEANINE. I thought advertising.

MARLENE. People often do think advertising. I have got a few vacancies but I think they're looking for something glossier.

JEANINE. You mean how I dress? / I can

MARLENE. I mean experience.

JEANINE. dress different. I dress like this on purpose for where I am now.

MARLENE. I have a marketing department here of a knitwear manufacturer. / Marketing is near enough

JEANINE. Knitwear?

MARLENE. advertising. Secretary to the marketing manager, he's thirty-five, married, I've sent him a girl before and she was happy, left to have a baby, you won't want to mention marriage there. He's very fair I think, good at his job, you won't have to nurse him along. Hundred and ten, so that's better than you're doing now.

JEANINE. I don't know.

MARLENE. I've a fairly small concern here, father and two sons, you'd have more say potentially, secretarial and reception duties, only a hundred but the job's going to grow with the concern and then you'll be in at the top with new girls coming in underneath you.

JEANINE. What is it they do?

MARLENE. Lampshades. / This would be my first choice for you.

JEANINE. Just lampshades?

MARLENE. There's plenty of different kinds of lampshade. So we'll send you there, shall we, and the knitwear second choice. Are you free to go for an interview any day they call you?

JEANINE. I'd like to travel.

MARLENE. We don't have any foreign clients. You'd have to go elsewhere.

JEANINE. Yes I know. I don't really . . . I just mean . . .

MARLENE. Does your fiancé want to travel?

JEANINE. I'd like a job where I was here in London and with him and everything but now and then — I expect it's silly. Are there jobs like that?

MARLENE. There's personal assistant to a top executive in a multinational. If that's the idea you need to be planning ahead. Is that where you want to be in ten years?

JEANINE. I might not be alive in ten years.

MARLENE. Yes but you will be. You'll have children.

JEANINE. I can't think about ten years.

MARLENE. You haven't got the speeds anyway. So I'll send you to these two shall I? You haven't been to any other agency? Just so we don't get crossed wires. Now,

Jeanine, I want you to get one of these jobs, all right? If I send you that means I'm putting myself on the line for you. Your presentation's OK, you look fine, just be confident and go in there convinced that this is the best job for you and you're the best person for the job. If you don't believe it they won't believe it.

JEANINE. Do you believe it?

MARLENE. I think you could make me believe it if you put your mind to it.

JEANINE. Yes, all right.

SCENE 3

JOYCE's back yard. Sunday afternoon. The house with a back door is us. ds. is a shelter made of junk, made by children. The Lights come up on two girls, ANGIE and KIT, who are squashed together in the shelter. ANGIE is sixteen, KIT is twelve. They cannot be seen from the house.

JOYCE. (*off, calling from the house*) Angie. Angie, are you out there?

(*Silence. They keep still and wait. When nothing else happens they relax.*)

ANGIE. Wish she was dead.

KIT. Wanna watch *The Exterminator?*

ANGIE. You're sitting on my leg.

KIT. There's nothing on telly. We can have an ice cream. Angie?

ANGIE. Shall I tell you something?

KIT. Do you wanna watch *The Exterminator?*

ANGIE. It's X, innit?

KIT. I can get into Xs.

ANGIE. Shall I tell you something?

KIT. We'll go to something else. We'll go to Ipswich. What's on the Odeon?

ANGIE. She won't let me, will she.

KIT. Don't tell her.

ANGIE. I've no money.

KIT. I'll pay.

ANGIE. She'll moan though, won't she.

KIT. I'll ask her for you if you like.

ANGIE. I've no money, I don't want you to pay.

KIT. I'll ask her.

ANGIE. She don't like you.

KIT. I still got three pounds birthday money. Did she say she don't like me? I'll go by myself then.

ANGIE. Your mum don't let you. I got to take you.

KIT. She won't know.

ANGIE. You'd be scared who'd sit next to you.

KIT. No I wouldn't. She does like me anyway. Tell me then.

ANGIE. Tell you what?

KIT. Its you she doesn't like.

ANGIE. Well I don't like her so tough shit.

JOYCE. (*off*) Angie. Angie. Angie. I know you're out there. I'm not coming out after you. You come in here. (*Silence. Nothing happens.*)

ANGIE. Last night when I was in bed. I been thinking yesterday could I make things move. You know, make things move by thinking about them without touching them. Last night I was in bed and suddenly a picture fell down off the wall.

KIT. What picture?

ANGIE. My gran, that picture. Not the poster. The photograph in the frame.

KIT. Had you done something to make it fall down?

ANGIE. I must have done.

KIT. But were you thinking about it?

ANGIE. Not about it, but about something.

KIT. I don't think that's very good.

ANGIE. You know the kitten?

KIT. Which one?

ANGIE. There only is one. The dead one.

KIT. What about it?

ANGIE. I heard it last night.

KIT. Where?

ANGIE. Out here. In the dark. What if I left you here in the dark all night?

KIT. You couldn't. I'd go home.

ANGIE. You couldn't.

KIT. I'd / go home.

ANGIE. No you couldn't, not if I said.

KIT. I could.

ANGIE. Then you wouldn't see anything. You'd just be ignorant.

KIT. I can see in the daytime.

ANGIE. No you can't. You can't hear it in the daytime.

KIT. I don't want to hear it.

ANGIE. You're scared that's all.

KIT. I'm not scared of anything.

ANGIE. You're scared of blood.

KIT. It's not the same kitten anyway. You just heard an old cat, / you just heard some old cat.

ANGIE. You don't know what I heard. Or what I saw. You don't know nothing because you're a baby.

KIT. You're sitting on me.

ANGIE. Mind my hair / you silly cunt.

KIT. Stupid fucking cow, I hate you.

ANGIE. I don't care if you do.

KIT. You're horrible.

ANGIE. I'm going to kill my mother and you're going to watch.

KIT. I'm not playing.

ANGIE. You're scared of blood. (*KIT puts her hand under dress, brings it out with blood on her finger.*)

KIT. There, see, I got my own blood, so. (*ANGIE takes KIT's hand and licks her finger.*)

ANGIE. Now I'm a cannibal. I might turn into a vampire now.

KIT. That picture wasn't nailed up right.

ANGIE. You'll have to do that when I get mine.

KIT. I don't have to.

ANGIE. You're scared.

KIT. I'll do it, I might do it. I don't have to just because you say. I'll be sick on you.

ANGIE. I don't care if you are sick on me, I don't mind sick. I don't mind blood. If I don't get away from here I'm going to die.

KIT. I'm going home.

ANGIE. You can't go through the house. She'll see you.

KIT. I won't tell her.

ANGIE. Oh great, fine.

KIT. I'll say I was by myself. I'll tell her you're at my house and I'm going there to get you.

ANGIE. She knows I'm here, stupid.

KIT. Then why can't I go through the house?

ANGIE. Because I said not.

KIT. My mum don't like you anyway.

ANGIE. I don't want her to like me. She's a slag.

KIT. She is not.

ANGIE. She does it with everyone.

KIT. She does not.

ANGIE. You don't even know what it is.

KIT. Yes I do.

ANGIE. Tell me then.

KIT. We get it all at school, cleverclogs. It's on television. You haven't done it.

ANGIE. How do you know?

KIT. Because I know you haven't.

ANGIE. You know wrong then because I have.

KIT. Who with?

ANGIE. I'm not telling you / who with.

KIT. You haven't anyway.

ANGIE. How do you know?

KIT. Who with?

ANGIE. I'm not telling you.

KIT. You said you told me everything.

ANGIE. I was lying wasn't I.

KIT. Who with? You can't tell me who with because / you never —

ANGIE. Sh.

(*JOYCE has come out of the house. She stops half way across the yard and listens. They listen.*)

JOYCE. You there Angie? Kit? You there Kitty? Want a cup of tea? I've got some chocolate biscuits. Come on now I'll put the kettle on. Want a choccy biccy, Angie? (*They all listen and wait.*) Fucking rotten little cunt. You can stay there and die. I'll lock the door.

(*They all wait. JOYCE goes back to the house. ANGIE and KIT sit in silence for a while.*)

KIT. When there's a war, where's the safest place?

ANGIE. Nowhere.

KIT. New Zealand is, my mum said. Your skin's burned right off. Shall we go to New Zealand?

ANGIE. I'm not staying here.

KIT. Shall we go to New Zealand?

ANGIE. You're not old enough.

KIT. You're not old enough.

ANGIE. I'm old enough to get married.

KIT. You don't want to get married.

ANGIE. No but I'm old enough.

KIT. I'd find out where they were going to drop it and stand right in the place.

ANGIE. You couldn't find out.

KIT. Better than walking round with your skin dragging on the ground. Eugh. / Would you like walking round with your skin dragging on the ground?

ANGIE. You couldn't find out, stupid, it's a secret.

KIT. Where are you going?

ANGIE. I'm not telling you.

KIT. Why?

ANGIE. It's a secret.

KIT. But you tell me all your secrets.

ANGIE. Not the true secrets.

KIT. Yes you do.

ANGIE. No I don't.

KIT. I want to go somewhere away from the war.

ANGIE. Just forget the war.

KIT. I can't.

ANGIE. You have to. It's so boring.

KIT. I'll remember it at night.

ANGIE. I'm going to do something else anyway.

KIT. What? Angie, come on. Angie.

ANGIE. It's a true secret.

KIT. It can't be worse than the kitten. And killing your mother. And the war.

ANGIE. Well I'm not telling you so you can die for all I care.

KIT. My mother says there's something wrong with you playing with someone my age. She says why haven't you got friends your own age. People your own age know there's something funny about you. She says you're a bad influence. She says she's going to speak to your mother. (*ANGIE twists KIT's arm till she cries out.*)

ANGIE. Say you're a liar.

KIT. She said it not me.

ANGIE. Say you eat shit.

KIT. You can't make me. (*ANGIE lets go.*)

ANGIE. I don't care anyway. I'm leaving.

KIT. Go on then.

ANGIE. You'll all wake up one morning and find I've gone.

KIT. Good.

ANGIE. I'm not telling you when.

KIT. Go on then.

ANGIE. I'm sorry I hurt you.

KIT. I'm tired.

ANGIE. Do you like me?

KIT. I don't know.

ANGIE. You do like me.

KIT. I'm going home. (*She gets up.*)

ANGIE. No you're not.

KIT. I'm tired.

ANGIE. She'll see you.

KIT. She'll give me a chocolate biscuit.

ANGIE. Kitty.

KIT. Tell me where you're going.

ANGIE. Sit down.

KIT. (*sitting down again*) Go on then.

ANGIE. Swear?

KIT. Swear.

ANGIE. I'm going to London. To see my aunt.

KIT. And what?

ANGIE. That's it.

KIT. I see my aunt all the time.

ANGIE. I don't see my aunt.

KIT. What's so special?

ANGIE. It is special. She's special.

KIT. Why?

ANGIE. She is.

KIT. Why?

ANGIE. She is.

KIT. Why?

ANGIE. My mother hates her.

KIT. Why?

ANGIE. Because she does.

KIT. Perhaps she's not very nice.

ANGIE. She is nice.

KIT. How do you know?

ANGIE. Because I know her.

KIT. You said you never see her.

ANGIE. I saw her last year. You saw her.

KIT. Did I?

ANGIE. Never mind.

KIT. I remember her. That aunt. What's so special?

ANGIE. She gets people jobs.

KIT. What's so special?

ANGIE. I think I'm my aunt's child. I think my mother's really my aunt.

KIT. Why?

ANGIE. Because she goes to America, now shut up.

KIT. I've been to London.

ANGIE. Now give us a cuddle and shut up because I'm
sick.

KIT. You're sitting on my arm.

(*They curl up in each other's arms. Silence. JOYCE
comes out of the house and comes up to them quietly.*)

JOYCE. Come on.

KIT. Oh hello.

JOYCE. Time you went home.

KIT. We want to go to the Odeon.

JOYCE. What time?

KIT. Don't know.

JOYCE. What's on?

KIT. Don't know.

JOYCE. Don't know much do you?

KIT. That all right then?

JOYCE. Angie's got to clean her room first.

ANGIE. No I don't.

JOYCE. Yes you do, it's a pigsty.

ANGIE. Well I'm not.

JOYCE. Then you're not going. I don't care.

ANGIE. Well I am going.

JOYCE. You've no money, have you?

ANGIE. Kit's paying anyway.

JOYCE. No she's not.

KIT. I'll help you with your room.

JOYCE. That's nice.

ANGIE. No you won't. You wait here.

KIT. Hurry then.

ANGIE. I'm not hurrying. You just wait. (*ANGIE
goes slowly into the house. Silence.*)

JOYCE. I don't know. (*silence*) How's school then?

KIT. All right.

JOYCE. What are you now? Third year?

KIT. Second year.

JOYCE. Your mum says you're good at English. (*silence*) Maybe Angie should've stayed on.

KIT. She didn't like it.

JOYCE. I didn't like it. And look at me. If your face fits at school it's going to fit other places too. It wouldn't make no difference to Angie. She's not going to get a job when jobs are hard to get. I'd be sorry for anyone in charge of her. She'd better get married. I don't know who'd have her, mind. She's one of those girls might never leave home. What do you want to be when you grow up, Kit?

KIT. Physicist.

JOYCE. What?

KIT. Nuclear physicist.

JOYCE. Whatever for?

KIT. I could, I'm clever.

JOYCE. I know you're clever, pet. (*silence*) I'll make a cup of tea. (*silence*) Looks like it's going to rain. (*silence*) Don't you have friends your own age?

KIT. Yes.

JOYCE. Well then.

KIT. I'm old for my age.

JOYCE. And Angie's si...ple is she? She's not simple.

KIT. I love Angie.

JOYCE. She's clever in her own way.

KIT. You can't stop me.

JOYCE. I don't want to.

KIT. You can't, so.

JOYCE. Don't be cheeky, Kitty. She's always kind to little children.

KIT. She's coming so you better leave me alone.

(*ANGIE comes out. She has changed into an old best dress, slightly small for her.*)

JOYCE. What you put that on for? Have you done your room? You can't clean you room in that.

ANGIE. I looked in the cupboard and it was there.

JOYCE. Of course it was there, it's meant to be there. Is that why it was a surprise, finding something in the right place? I should think she's surprised, wouldn't you, Kit, to find something in her room in the right place.

ANGIE. I decided to wear it.

JOYCE. Not today, why? To clean your room? You're not going to the pictures till you've done your room. You can put your dress on after if you like. (*ANGIE picks up a brick.*) Have you done your room? You're not getting out of it, you know.

KIT. Angie, let's go.

JOYCE. She's not going till she's done her room.

KIT. It's starting to rain.

JOYCE. Come on, come on then. Hurry and do your room, Angie, and then you can go to the cinema with Kit. Oh it's wet, come on. We'll look up the time in the paper. Does your mother know, Kit, it's going to be a late night for you, isn't it? Hurry up, Angie. You'll spoil your dress. You make me sick. (*JOYCE and KIT run into the house. ANGIE stays where she is. There is the sound of rain. KIT comes out of the house.*)

KIT. (*shouting*) Angie. Angie, come on, you'll get wet. (*She comes back to ANGIE.*)

ANGIE. I put on this dress to kill my mother.

KIT. I suppose you thought you'd do it with a brick.

ANGIE. You can kill people with a brick. (*She puts the brick down.*)

KIT. Well you didn't, so.

ACT TWO

SCENE 1

*"Top Girls" Employment Agency. Monday morning.
There are three desks in the main office and a
separate small interviewing area. The Lights come
up in the main office on WIN and NELL who have
just arrived for work.*

NELL. Coffee coffee coffee coffee / coffee.

WIN. The roses were smashing. / Mermaid.

NELL. Ohhh.

WIN. Iceberg. He taught me all their names. (*NELL
has some coffee now.*)

NELL. Ah. Now then.

WIN. He has one of the finest rose gardens in West
Sussex. He exhibits.

NELL. He what?

WIN. His wife was visiting her mother. It was like living together.

NELL. Crafty, you never said.

WIN. He rang on Saturday morning.

NELL. Lucky you were free.

WIN. That's what I told him.

NELL. Did you hell.

WIN. Have you ever seen a really beautiful rose
garden?

NELL. I don't like flowers. / I like swimming pools.

WIN. Marilyn. Esther's Baby. They're all called after
birds.

NELL. Our friend's late. Celebrating all weekend I bet
you.

WIN. I'd call a rose Elvis. Or John Conteh.

NELL. Is Howard in yet?

56

WIN. If he is he'll be bleeping us with a problem.

NELL. Howard can just hang on to himself.

WIN. Howard's really cut up.

NELL. Howard thinks because he's a fella the job was his as of right. Our Marlene's got far more balls than Howard and that's that.

WIN. Poor little bugger.

NELL. He'll live.

WIN. He'll move on.

NELL. I wouldn't mind a change of air myself.

WIN. Serious?

NELL. I've never been a staying-put lady. Pastures new.

WIN. So who's the pirate?

NELL. There's nothing definite.

WIN. Inquiries?

NELL. There's always inquiries. I'd think I'd got bad breath if there stopped being inquiries. Most of them can't afford me. Or you.

WIN. I'm all right for the time being. Unless I go to Australia.

NELL. There's not a lot of room upward.

WIN. Marlene's filled it up.

NELL. Good luck to her. Unless there's some prospects moneywise.

WIN. You can but ask.

NELL. Can always but ask.

WIN. So what have we got? I've got a Mr Holden I saw last week.

NELL. Any use?

WIN. Pushy. Bit of a cowboy.

NELL. Goodlooker?

WIN. Good dresser.

NELL. High flyer?

WIN. That's his general idea certainly but I'm not sure he's got it up there.

NELL. Prestel wants six flyers and I've only seen two and a half.

WIN. He's making a bomb on the road but he thinks it's time for an office. I sent him to IBM but he didn't get it.

NELL. Prestel's on the road.

WIN. He's not overbright.

NELL. Can he handle an office?

WIN. Provided his secretary can punctuate he should go far.

NELL. Bear Prestel in mind then, I might put my head round the door. I've got that poor little nerd I should never had said I could help. Tender heart me.

WIN. Tender like old boots. How old?

NELL. Yes well forty-five.

WIN. Say no more.

NELL. He knows his place, he's not after calling himself a manager, he's just a poor little bod wants a better commission and a bit of sunshine.

WIN. Don't we all.

NELL. He's just got to relocate. He's got a bungalow in Dymchurch.

WIN. And his wife says.

NELL. The lady wife wouldn't care to relocate. She's going through the change.

WIN. It's his funeral, don't waste your time.

NELL. I don't waste a lot.

WIN. Good weekend you?

NELL. You could say.

WIN. Which one?

NELL. One Friday, one Saturday.

WIN. Aye—aye.

NELL. Sunday night I watched telly.

WIN. Which of them do you like best really?

NELL. Sunday was best, I like the Ovaltine.

WIN. Holden, Barker, Gardner, Duke.

NELL. I've a lady here thinks she can sell.

WIN. Taking her on?

NELL. She's had some jobs.

WIN. Services?

NELL. No, quite heavy stuff, electric.

WIN. Tough bird like us.

NELL. We could do with a few more here.

WIN. There's nothing going here.

NELL. No but I always want the tough ones when I see them. Hang on to them.

WIN. I think we're plenty.

NELL. Derek asked me to marry him again.

WIN. He doesn't know when he's beaten.

NELL. I told him I'm not going to play house, not even in Ascot.

WIN. Mind you, you could play house.

NELL. If I chose to play house I would play house ace.

WIN. You could marry him and go on working.

NELL. I could go on working and not marry him.

(*MARLENE arrives.*)

MARLENE. Morning ladies. (*WIN and NELL cheer and whistle.*) Mind my head.

NELL. Coffee coffee coffee.

WIN. We're tactfully not mentioning you're late.

MARLENE. Fucking tube.

WIN. We've heard that one.

NELL. We've used that one.

WIN. It's the top executive doesn't come in as early as the poor working girl.

MARLENE. Pass the sugar and shut your face, pet.

WIN. Well I'm delighted.

NELL. Howard's looking sick.

WIN. Howard is sick. He's got ulcers and heart. He told me.

NELL. He'll have to stop then, won't he?

WIN. Stop what?

NELL. Smoking, drinking, shouting. Working.

WIN. Well, working.

NELL. We're just looking through the day.

MARLENE. I'm doing some of Pam's ladies. They've been piling up while she's away.

NELL. Half a dozen little girls and an arts graduate who can't type.

WIN. I spent the whole weekend at his place in Sussex.

NELL. She fancies his rose garden.

WIN. I had to lie down in the back of the car so the neighbours wouldn't see me go in.

NELL. You're kidding.

WIN. It was funny.

NELL. Fuck that for a joke.

WIN. It was funny.

MARLENE. Anyway they'd see you in the garden.

WIN. The garden has extremely high walls.

NELL. I think I'll tell the wife.

WIN. Like hell.

NELL. She might leave him and you could have the rose garden.

WIN. The minute it's not a secret I'm out on my ear.

NELL. Don't know why you bother.

WIN. Bit of fun.

NELL. I think it's time you went to Australia.

WIN. I think it's pushy Mr Holden time.

NELL. If you've any really pretty bastards, Marlene, I want some for Prestel.

MARLENE. I might have one this afternoon. This morning it's all Pam's secretarial.

NELL. Not long now and you'll be upstairs watching over us all.

MARLENE. Do you fell bad about it?

NELL. I don't like coming second.

MARLENE. Who does?

WIN. We'd rather it was you than Howard. We're glad for you, aren't we, Nell?

NELL. Oh yes. Aces.

(*LOUISE enters the interviewing area. The Lights crossfade to WIN and LOUISE in the interviewing area. NELL exits.*)

WIN. Now, Louise, hello, I have your details here. You've been very loyal to the one job I see.

LOUISE. Yes I have.

WIN. Twenty-one years is a long time in one place.

LOUISE. I feel it is. I feel it's time to move on.

WIN. And you are what age now?

LOUISE. I'm in my early forties.

WIN. Exactly?

LOUISE. Forty-six.

WIN. It's not necessarily a handicap, well it is of course we have to face that, but it's not necessarily a disabling handicap, experience does count for something.

LOUISE. I hope so.

WIN. Now between ourselves is there any trouble, any reason why you're leaving that wouldn't appear on the form?

LOUISE. Nothing like that.

WIN. Like what?

LOUISE. Nothing at all.

WIN. No long term understandings come to a sudden end, making for an insupportable atmosphere?

LOUISE. I've always completely avoided anything like that at all.

WIN. No personality clashes with your immediate superiors or inferiors?

LOUISE. I've always taken care to get on very well with everyone.

WIN. I only ask because it can affect the reference and it also affects your motivation, I want to be quite clear why you're moving on. So I take it the job itself no longer satisfies you. Is it the money?

LOUISE. It's partly the money. It's not so much the money.

WIN. Nine thousand is very respectable. Have you dependants?

LOUISE. No, no dependants. My mother died.

WIN. So why are you making a change?

LOUISE. Other people make changes.

WIN. But why are you, now, after spending most of your life in the one place?

LOUISE. There you are, I've lived for that company, I've given my life really you could say because I haven't had a great deal of social life, I've worked in the evenings. I haven't had office entanglements for the very reason you just mentioned and if you are committed to your work you don't move in many other circles. I had management status from the age of twenty-seven and you'll appreciate what that means. I've built up a department. And there it is, it works extremely well, and I feel I'm stuck there. I've spent twenty years in middle management. I've seen young men who I trained go on, in my own company or elsewhere, to higher things. Nobody notices me, I don't expect it, I don't attract attention by making mistakes, everybody takes it for granted that my work is perfect. They will notice me when I go, they will be sorry I think to lose me, they will offer me more money of course, I will refuse. They will see when I've gone what I was doing for them.

WIN. If they offer you more money you won't stay?

LOUISE. No I won't.

WIN. Are you the only woman?

LOUISE. Apart from the girls of course, yes. There was one, she was my assistant, it was the only time I took on a young woman assistant, I always had my doubts. I don't care greatly for working with women, I think I pass as a man at work. But I did take on this young woman, her qualifications were excellent, and she did well, she got a department of her own, and left the company for a competitor where she's now on the board and good luck to her. She has a different style, she's a new kind of attractive well-dressed — I don't mean I don't dress properly. But there is a kind of woman who is thirty now who grew up in a different climate. They are not so careful. They take themselves for granted. I have had to justify my existence every minute, and I have done so, I have proved — well.

WIN. Let's face it, vacancies are ones where you'll be in competition with younger men. And there are companies that will value your experience enough that you'll be in with a chance. There are also fields that are easier for a woman, there is a cosmetic company here where your experience might be relevant. It's eight and a half, I don't know if that appeals.

LOUISE. I've proved I can earn money. It's more important to get away. I feel it's now or never. I sometimes / think—

WIN. You shouldn't talk too much at an interview.

LOUISE. I don't. I don't normally talk about myself. I know very well how to handle myself in an office situation. I only talk to you because it seems to me this is different, it's your job to understand me, surely. You asked the questions.

WIN. I think I understand you sufficiently.

LOUISE. Well good, that's good.

WIN. Do you drink?

LOUISE. Certainly not. I'm not a teetotaller, I think that's very suspect, it's seen as being an alcoholic if you're teetotal. What do you mean? I don't drink. Why?

WIN. I drink.

LOUISE. I don't.

WIN. Good for you.

(*The Lights crossfade to the main office with MAR-LENE sitting at her desk. WIN and LOUISE exit. ANGIE arrives in the main office.*)

ANGIE. Hello.

MARLENE. Have you an appointment?

ANGIE. It's me. I've come.

MARLENE. What? It's not Angie?

ANGIE. It was hard to find this place. I got lost.

MARLENE. How did you get past the receptionist? The girl on the desk, didn't she try to stop you?

ANGIE. What desk?

MARLENE. Never mind.

ANGIE. I just walked in. I was looking for you.

MARLENE. Well you found me.

ANGIE. Yes.

MARLENE. So where's your mum? Are you up in town for the day?

ANGIE. Not really.

MARLENE. Sit down. Do you feel all right?

ANGIE. Yes thank you.

MARLENE. So where's Joyce?

ANGIE. She's at home.

MARLENE. Did you come up on a school trip then?

ANGIE. I've left school.

MARLENE. Did you come up with a friend?

ANGIE. No. There's just me.

MARLENE. You came up by yourself, that's fun. What have you been doing? Shopping? Tower of London?

ANGIE. No, I just come here. I come to you.

MARLENE. That's very nice of you to think of paying your aunty a visit. There's not many nieces make that the first port of call. Would you like a cup of coffee?

ANGIE. No thank you.

MARLENE. Tea, orange?

ANGIE. No thank you.

MARLENE. Do you feel all right?

ANGIE. Yes thank you.

MARLENE. Are you tired from the journey?

ANGIE. Yes, I'm tired from the journey.

MARLENE. You sit there for a bit then. How's Joyce?

ANGIE. She's all right.

MARLENE. Same as ever.

ANGIE. Oh yes.

MARLENE. Unfortunately you've picked a day when I'm rather busy, if there's ever a day when I'm not, or I'd take you out to lunch and we'd go to Madame Tussaud's. We could go shopping. What time do you have to be back? Have you got a day return?

ANGIE. No.

MARLENE. So what train are you going back on?

ANGIE. I came on the bus.

MARLENE. So what bus are you going back on? Are you staying the night?

ANGIE. Yes.

MARLENE. Who are you staying with? Do you want me to put you up for the night, is that it?

ANGIE. Yes please.

MARLENE. I haven't got a spare bed.

ANGIE. I can sleep on the floor.

MARLENE. You can sleep on the sofa.

ANGIE. Yes please.

MARLENE. I do think Joyce might have phoned me. It's like her.

ANGIE. This is where you work is it?

MARLENE. It's where I have been working the last two years but I'm going to move into another office.

ANGIE. It's lovely.

MARLENE. My new office is nicer than this. There's just the one big desk in it for me.

ANGIE. Can I see it?

MARLENE. Not now, no, there's someone else in it now. But he's leaving at the end of next week and I'm going to do his job.

ANGIE. Is that good?

MARLENE. Yes, it's very good.

ANGIE. Are you going to be in charge?

MARLENE. Yes I am.

ANGIE. I knew you would be.

MARLENE. How did you know?

ANGIE. I knew you'd be in charge of everything.

MARLENE. Not quite everything.

ANGIE. You will be.

MARLENE. Well we'll see.

ANGIE. Can I see it next week then?

MARLENE. Will you still be here next week?

ANGIE. Yes.

MARLENE. Don't you have to go home?

ANGIE. No.

MARLENE. Why not?

ANGIE. It's all right.

MARLENE. Is it all right?

ANGIE. Yes, don't worry about it.

MARLENE. Does Joyce know where you are?

ANGIE. Yes of course she does.

MARLENE. Well does she?

ANGIE. Don't worry about it.

MARLENE. How long are you planning to stay with me then?

ANGIE. You know when you came to see us last year?

MARLENE. Yes, that was nice wasn't it.

ANGIE. That was the best day of my whole life.

MARLENE. So how long are you planning to stay?

ANGIE. Don't you want me?

MARLENE. Yes yes, I just wondered.

ANGIE. I won't stay if you don't want me.

MARLENE. No, of course you can stay.

ANGIE. I'll sleep on the floor. I won't be any bother.

MARLENE. Don't get upset.

ANGIE. I'm not, I'm not. Don't worry about it.

(MRS KIDD comes in.)

MRS KIDD. Excuse me.

MARLENE. Yes.

MRS KIDD. Excuse me.

MARLENE. Can I help you?

MRS KIDD. Excuse me bursting in on you like this but I have to talk to you.

MARLENE. I am engaged at the moment. / If you could go to reception—

MRS KIDD. I'm Rosemary Kidd, Howard's wife, you don't recognize me but we did meet, I remember you of course / but you wouldn't—

MARLENE. Yes of course, Mrs Kidd, I'm sorry, we did meet. Howard's about somewhere I expect, have you looked in his office?

MRS KIDD. Howard's not about, no. I'm afraid it's you I've come to see if I could have a minute or two.

MARLENE. I do have an appointment in five minutes.

MRS KIDD. This won't take five minutes. I'm very sorry. It is a matter of some urgency.

MARLENE. Well of course. What can I do for you?

MRS KIDD. I just wanted a chat, an informal chat. It's not something I can simply—I'm sorry if I'm interrupting your work. I know office work isn't like housework / which is all interruptions.

MARLENE. No no, this is my niece. Angie. Mrs Kidd.

MRS KIDD. Very pleased to meet you.

ANGIE. Very well thank you.

MRS KIDD. Howard's not in today.

MARLENE. Isn't he?

MRS KIDD. He's feeling poorly.

MARLENE. I didn't know. I'm sorry to hear that.

MRS KIDD. The fact is he's in a state of shock. About what's happened.

MARLENE. What has happened?

MRS KIDD. You should know if anyone. I'm referring to you been appointed managing director instead of Howard. He hasn't been at all well all weekend. He hasn't slept for three nights. I haven't slept.

MARLENE. I'm sorry to hear that, Mrs Kidd. Has he thought of taking sleeping pills?

MRS KIDD. It's very hard when someone has worked all these years.

MARLENE. Business life is full of little setbacks. I'm sure Howard knows that. He'll bounce back in a day or two. We all bounce back.

MRS KIDD. If you could see him you'd know what I'm talking about. What's it going to do to him working for a woman? I think if it was a man he'd get over it as something normal.

MARLENE. I think he's going to have to get over it.

MRS KIDD. It's me that bears the brunt. I'm not the one that's been promoted. I put him first every inch of the way. And now what do I get? You women this, you women that. It's not my fault. You're going to have to be very careful how you handle him. He's very hurt.

MARLENE. Naturally I'll be tactful and pleasant to him, you don't start pushing someone around. I'll consult him over any decisions affecting his department. But that's no different, Mrs Kidd, from any of my other colleagues.

MRS KIDD. I think it is different, because he's a man.

MARLENE. I'm not quite sure why you came to see me.

MRS KIDD. I had to do something.

MARLENE. Well you've done it, you've seen me. I think that's probably all we've time for. I'm sorry he's been taking it out on you. He really is a shit, Howard.

MRS KIDD. But he's got a family to support. He's got three children. It's only fair.

MARLENE. Are you suggesting I give up the job to him then?

MRS KIDD. It had crossed my mind if you were unavailable after all for some reason, he would be the natural second choice I think, don't you? I'm not asking.

MARLENE. Good.

MRS KIDD. You mustn't tell him I came. He's very proud.

MARLENE. If he doesn't like what's happening here he can go and work somewhere else.

MRS KIDD. Is that a threat?

MARLENE. I'm sorry but I do have some work to do.

MRS KIDD. It's not that easy, a man of Howard's age. You don't care. I thought he was going too far but he's right. You're one of these ballbreakers, / that's what you

MARLENE. I'm sorry but I do have some work to do.

MRS KIDD. are. You'll end up miserable and lonely. You're not natural.

MARLENE. Could you please piss off?

MRS KIDD. I thought if I saw you at least I'd be doing something. (*MRS KIDD goes.*)

MARLENE. I've got to go and do some work now. Will you come back later?

ANGIE. I think you were wonderful.

MARLENE. I've got to go and do some work now.

ANGIE. You told her to piss off.

MARLENE. Will you come back later?

ANGIE. Can't I stay here?

MARLENE. Don't you want to go sightseeing?

ANGIE. I'd rather stay here.

MARLENE. You can stay here I suppose, if it's not boring.

ANGIE. It's where I most want to be in the world.

MARLENE. I'll see you later then.

(*MARLENE goes. SHONA and NELL enter the interviewing area. ANGIE sits at WIN's desk. The
Lights crossfade to NELL and SHONA in the interviewing area.*)

NELL. Is this right? You are Shona?

SHONA. Yeh.

NELL. It says here you're twenty-nine.

SHONA. Yeh.

NELL. Too many late nights, me. So you've been
where you are for four years, Shona, you're earning six
basic and three commission. So what's the problem?

SHONA. No problem.

NELL. Why do you want a change?

SHONA. Just a change.

NELL. Change of product, change of area?

SHONA. Both.

NELL. But you're happy on the road?

SHONA. I like driving.

NELL. You're not after management status?

SHONA. I would like management status.

NELL. You'd be interested in titular management
status but not come off the road?

SHONA. I want to be on the road, yeh.

NELL. So how many calls have you been making a
day?

SHONA. Six.

NELL. And what proportion of those are successful?

SHONA. Six.

NELL. That's hard to believe.

SHONA. Four.

NELL. You find it easy to get the initial interest do you?

SHONA. Oh yeh, I get plenty of initial interest.

NELL. And what about closing?

SHONA. I close, don't I?

NELL. Because that's what an employer is going to have doubts about with a lady as I needn't tell you, whether she's got the guts to push through to a closing situation. They think we're too nice. They think we listen to the buyer's doubts. They think we consider his needs and his feelings.

SHONA. I never consider people's feelings.

NELL. I was selling for six years, I can sell anything, I've sold in three continents, and I'm jolly as they come but I'm not very nice.

SHONA. I'm not very nice.

NELL. What sort of time do you have on the road with the other reps? Get on all right? Handle the chat?

SHONA. I get on. Keep myself to myself.

NELL. Fairly much of a loner are you?

SHONA. Sometimes.

NELL. So what field are you interested in?

SHONA. Computers.

NELL. That's a top field as you know and you'll be up against some very slick fellas there, there's some very pretty boys in computers, it's an American-style field.

SHONA. That's why I want to do it.

NELL. Video systems appeal? That's a high-flying situation.

SHONA. Video systems appeal OK.

NELL. Because Prestel have half a dozen vacancies I'm looking to fill at the moment. We're talking in the area of ten to fifteen thousand here and upwards.

SHONA. Sounds OK.

NELL. I've half a mind to go for it myself. But it's good money here if you've got the top clients. Could you fancy it do you think?

SHONA. Work here?

NELL. I'm not in a positon to offer, there's nothing officially going just now, but we're always on the lookout. There's not that many of us. We could keep in touch.

SHONA. I like driving.

NELL. So the Prestel appeals?

SHONA. Yeh.

NELL. What about ties?

SHONA. No ties.

NELL. So relocation wouldn't be a problem.

SHONA. No problem.

NELL. So just fill me in a bit more could you about what you've been doing.

SHONA. What I've been doing. It's all down there.

NELL. The bare facts are down here but I've got to present you to an employer.

SHONA. I'm twenty-nine years old.

NELL. So it says here.

SHONA. We look young. Youngness runs in the family in our family.

NELL. So just describe your present job for me.

SHONA. My present job at present. I have a car. I have a Porsche. I go up the M1 a lot. Burn up the M1 a lot. Straight up the M1 in the fast lane to where the clients are, Staffordshire, Yorkshire, I do a lot in Yorkshire. I'm selling electric things. Like dishwashers, washing machines, stainless steel tubs are a feature and the reliability of the programme. After sales service, we offer a very good after sales service, spare parts, plenty of spare parts. And fridges, I sell a lot of fridges specially in the summer. People want to buy fridges in the sum-

mer because of the heat melting the butter and you get
fed up standing the milk in a basin of cold water with a
cloth over, stands to reason people don't want to do that
in this day and age. So I sell a lot of them. Big ones with
big freezers. Big freezers. And I stay in hotels at night
when I'm away from home. On my expense account. I
stay in various hotels. They know me, the ones I go to. I
check in, have a bath, have a shower. Then I go down to
the bar, have a gin and tonic, have a chat. Then I go into
the dining room and have dinner. I usually have fillet
steak and mushrooms, I like mushrooms. I like smoked
salmon very much. I like having a salad on the side.
Green salad. I don't like tomatoes.

NELL. Christ what a waste of time.

SHONA. Beg your pardon?

NELL. Not a word of this is true, is it?

SHONA. How do you mean?

NELL. You just filled in the form with a pack of lies.

SHONA. Not exactly.

NELL. How old are you?

SHONA. Twenty-nine.

NELL. Nineteen?

SHONA. Twenty-one.

NELL. And what jobs have you done? Have you done
any?

SHONA. I could though, I bet you.

(*The Lights crossfade to the main office with ANGIE
sitting as before. WIN comes in to the main office.
SHONA and NELL exit.*)

WIN. Who's sitting in my chair?

ANGIE. What? Sorry.

WIN. Who's been eating my porridge?

ANGIE. What?

WIN. It's all right, I saw Marlene. Angie, isn't it? I'm Win. And I'm not going out for lunch because I'm knackered. I'm going to set me down here and have a yoghurt. Do you like yoghurt?

ANGIE. No.

WIN. That's good because I've only got one. Are you hungry?

ANGIE. No.

WIN. There's a cafe on the corner.

ANGIE. No thank you. Do you work here?

WIN. How did you guess?

ANGIE. Because you look as if you might work here and you're sitting at the desk. Have you always worked here?

WIN. No I was headhunted. That means I was working for another outfit like this and this lot came and offered me more money. I broke my contract, there was a hell of a stink. There's not many top ladies about. Your aunty's a smashing bird.

ANGIE. Yes I know.

MARLENE. Fan are you? Fan of your aunty's?

ANGIE. Do you think I could work here?

WIN. Not at the moment.

ANGIE. How do I start?

WIN. What can you do?

ANGIE. I don't know. Nothing.

WIN. Type?

ANGIE. Not very well. The letters jump up when I do capitals. I was going to do a CSE in commerce but I didn't.

WIN. What have you got?

ANGIE. What?

WIN. CSE's, O's.

ANGIE. Nothing, none of that. Did you do all that?

WIN. Oh yes, all that, and a science degree funnily enough. I started out doing medical research but there's no money in it. I thought I'd go abroad. Did you know they sell Coca Cola in Russia and Pepsi-Cola in China? You don't have to be qualified as much as you might think. Men are awful bullshitters, they like to make out jobs are harder than they are. Any job I ever did I started doing it better than the rest of the crowd and they didn't like it. So I'd get unpopular and I'd have a drink to cheer myself up. I lived with a fella and supported him for four years, he couldn't get work. After that I went to California. I like the sunshine. Americans know how to live. This country's too slow. Then I went to Mexico, still in sales, but it's no country for a single lady. I came home, went bonkers for a bit, thought I was five different people, got over that all right, the psychiatrist said I was perfectly sane and highly intelligent. Got married in a moment of weakness and he's inside now, he's been inside four years, and I've not been to see him too much this last year. I like this better than sales, I'm not really that aggressive. I started thinking sales was a good job if you want to meet people, but you're meeting people that don't want to meet you. It's no good if you like being liked. Here your clients want to meet you because you're the one doing them some good. They hope. (*ANGIE has fallen asleep. NELL comes in.*)

NELL. You're talking to yourself, sunshine.

WIN. So what's new?

NELL. Who is this?

WIN. Marlene's little niece.

NELL. What's she got, brother, sister? She never talks about her family.

WIN. I was telling her my life story.

NELL. Violins?

WIN. No, success story.

NELL. You've heard Howard's had a heart attack?

WIN. No, when?

NELL. I heard just now. He hadn't come in, he was at home, he's gone to hospital. He's not dead. His wife was here, she rushed off in a cab.

WIN. Too much butter, too much smoke. We must send him some flowers. (*MARLENE comes in.*) You've heard about Howard?

MARLENE. Poor sod.

NELL. Lucky he didn't get the job if that's what his health's like.

MARLENE. Is she asleep?

WIN. She wants to work here.

MARLENE. Packer in Tesco more like.

WIN. She's a nice kid. Isn't she?

MARLENE. She's a bit thick. She's a bit funny.

WIN. She thinks you're wonderful.

MARLENE. She's not going to make it.

SCENE 2

JOYCE's kitchen. Sunday evening, a year earlier. The Lights come up on JOYCE, ANGIE and MAR-LENE. MARLENE is taking presents out of bright carrier bag. ANGIE has already opened a box of chocolates.

MARLENE. Just a few little things. / I've

JOYCE. There's no need.

MARLENE. no memory for birthdays have I, and

Christmas seems to slip by. So I think I owe Angie a few presents.

JOYCE. What do you say?

ANGIE. Thank you very much. Thank you very much, Aunty Marlene. (*She opens a present. It is the dress from Act One, new.*) Oh look, Mum, isn't it lovely?

MARLENE. I don't know if it's the right size. She's grown up since I saw her. / I knew she was always

ANGIE. Isn't it lovely?

MARLENE. tall for her age.

JOYCE. She's a big lump.

MARLENE. Hold it up, Angie, let's see.

ANGIE. I'll put it on, shall I?

MARLENE. Yes, try it on.

JOYCE. Go on to your room then, we don't want / a strip show thank you.

ANGIE. Of course I'm going to my room, what do you think. Look, Mum, here's something for you. Open it, go on. What is it? Can I open it for you?

JOYCE. Yes, you open it, pet.

ANGIE. Don't you want to open it yourself? / Go on.

JOYCE. I don't mind, you can do it.

ANGIE. It's something hard. It's—what is it? A bottle. Drink is it? No, it's what? Perfume, look. What a lot. Open it, look, let's smell it. Oh it's strong. It's lovely. Put it on me. How do you do it? Put it on me.

JOYCE. You're too young.

ANGIE. I can play wearing it like dressing up.

JOYCE. And you're too old for that. Here, give it here, I'll do it, you'll tip the whole bottle over yourself / and we'll have you smelling all summer.

ANGIE. Put it on you. Do I smell? Put it on Aunty too. Put it on Aunty too. Let's all smell.

MARLENE. I didn't know what you'd like.

JOYCE. There's no danger I'd have it already, / that's one thing.

ANGIE. Now we all smell the same.

MARLENE. It's a bit of nonsense.

JOYCE. It's very kind of you Marlene, you shouldn't.

ANGIE. Now I'll put on the dress and then we'll see. (*ANGIE goes.*)

JOYCE. You've caught me on the hop with the place in the mess. / If you'd let me

MARLENE. That doesn't matter.

JOYCE. know you was coming I'd have got something in to eat. We had our dinner dinnertime. We're just going to have a cup of tea. You could have an egg.

MARLENE. No, I'm not hungry. Tea's fine.

JOYCE. I don't expect you take sugar.

MARLENE. Why not?

JOYCE. You take care of yourself.

MARLENE. How do you mean you didn't know I was coming?

JOYCE. You could have written. I know we're not on the phone but we're not completely in the dark ages, / we do have a postman.

MARLENE. But you asked me to come.

JOYCE. How did I ask you to come?

MARLENE. Angie said when she phoned up.

JOYCE. Angie phoned up, did she.

MARLENE. Was it just Angie's idea?

JOYCE. What did she say?

MARLENE. She said you wanted me to come and see you. / It was a couple of

JOYCE. Ha.

MARLENE. weeks ago. How was I to know that's a ridiculous idea? My diary's always full a couple of weeks ahead so we fixed it for this weekend. I was meant to get here earlier but I was held up. She gave me messages from you.

JOYCE. Didn't you wonder why I didn't phone you myself?

MARLENE. She said you didn't like using the phone. You're shy on the phone and can't use it. I don't know what you're like, do I?

JOYCE. Are there people who can't use the phone?

MARLENE. I expect so.

JOYCE. I haven't met any.

MARLENE. Why should I think she was lying?

JOYCE. Because she's like what she's like.

MARLENE. How do I know / what she's like?

JOYCE. It's not my fault you don't know what she's like. You never come and see her.

MARLENE. Well I have now / and you don't seem over the moon.*

JOYCE. Good. *Well I'd have got a cake if she'd told me. (*pause*)

MARLENE. I did wonder why you wanted to see me.

JOYCE. I didn't want to see you.

MARLENE. Yes, I know. Shall I go?

JOYCE. I don't mind seeing you.

MARLENE. Great, I feel really welcome.

JOYCE. You can come and see Angie any time you like, I'm not stopping you. / You

MARLENE. Ta ever so.

JOYCE. know where we are. You're the one went away, not me. I'm right here where I was. And will be a few years yet I shouldn't wonder.

MARLENE. All right. All right. (*JOYCE gives MARLENE a cup of tea.*)

JOYCE. Tea.

MARLENE. Sugar? (*JOYCE passes MARLENE the sugar.*) It's very quiet down here.

JOYCE. I expect you'd notice it.

MARLENE. The air smells different too.

JOYCE. That's the scent.

MARLENE. No, I mean walking down the lane.

JOYCE. What sort of air you get in London then?

(*ANGIE comes in, wearing the dress. It fits.*)

MARLENE. Oh, very pretty. / You do look pretty, Angie.

JOYCE. That fits all right.

MARLENE. Do you like the colour?

ANGIE. Beautiful. Beautiful.

JOYCE. You better take it off, / you'll get it dirty.

ANGIE. I want to wear it. I want to wear it.

MARLENE. It is for wearing after all. You can't just hang it up and look at it.

ANGIE. I love it.

JOYCE. Well if you must you must.

ANGIE. If someone asks me what's my favourite colour I'll tell them it's this. Thank you very much, Aunty Marlene.

MARLENE. You didn't tell your mum you asked me down.

ANGIE. I wanted it to be a surprise.

JOYCE. I'll give you a surprise / one of these days.

ANGIE. I thought you'd like to see her. She hasn't been here since I was nine. People do see their aunts.

MARLENE. Is it that long? Doesn't time fly.

ANGIE. I wanted to.

JOYCE. I'm not cross.

ANGIE. Are you glad?

JOYCE. I smell nicer anyhow, don't I?

(*KIT comes in without saying anything, as if she lived there.*)

MARLENE. I think it was a good idea, Angie, about time. We are sisters after all. It's a pity to let that go.

JOYCE. This is Kitty, / who lives up the road. This is Angie's Aunty Marlene.

KIT. What's that?

ANGIE. It's a present. Do you like it?

KIT. It's all right. / Are you coming out?*

MARLENE. Hello, Kitty.

ANGIE. *No.

KIT. What's that smell?

ANGIE. It's a present.

KIT. It's horrible. Come on.*

MARLENE. Have a chocolate.

ANGIE. *No, I'm busy.

KIT. Coming out later?

ANGIE. No.

KIT. (*to MARLENE*) Hello. (*KIT goes without a chocolate.*)

JOYCE. She's a little girl Angie sometimes plays with because she's the only child lives really close. She's like a little sister to her really. Angie's good with little children.

MARLENE. Do you want to work with children, Angie? / Be a teacher or a nursery nurse?

JOYCE. I don't think she's ever thought of it.

MARLENE. What do you want to do?

JOYCE. She hasn't an idea in her head what she wants to do. / Lucky to get anything.

MARLENE. Angie?

JOYCE. She's not clever like you. (*pause*)

MARLENE. I'm not clever, just pushy.

JOYCE. True enough. (*MARLENE takes a bottle of whisky out of the bag.*) I don't drink spirits.

ANGIE. You do at Christmas.

JOYCE. It's not Christmas, is it?

ANGIE. It's better than Christmas.

MARLENE. Glasses?

JOYCE. Just a small one then.

MARLENE. Do you want some, Angie?

ANGIE. I can't, can I?

JOYCE. Taste it if you want. You won't like it. (*ANGIE tastes it.*)

ANGIE. Mmm.

MARLENE. We got drunk together the night your grandfather died.

JOYCE. We did not get drunk.

MARLENE. I got drunk. You were just overcome with grief.

JOYCE. I still keep up the grave with flowers.

MARLENE. Do you really?

JOYCE. Why wouldn't I?

MARLENE. Have you seen Mother?

JOYCE. Of course I've seen Mother.

MARLENE. I mean lately.

JOYCE. Of course I've seen her lately, I go every Thursday.

MARLENE. (*to ANGIE*) Do you remember your grandfather?

ANGIE. He got me out of the bath one night in a towel.

MARLENE. Did he? I don't think he ever gave me a bath. Did he give you a bath, Joyce? He probably got soft in his old age. Did you like him?

ANGIE. Yes of course.

MARLENE. Why?

ANGIE. What?

MARLENE. So what's the news? How's Mrs Paisley? Still going crazily? / And Dorothy. What happened to Dorothy?*

ANGIE. Who's Mrs Paisley?

JOYCE. *She went to Canada.

MARLENE. Did she? What to do?

JOYCE. I don't know. She just went to Canada.

MARLENE. Well / good for her.

ANGIE. Mr Connolly killed his wife.

MARLENE. What, Connolly at Whitegates?

ANGIE. They found her body in the garden. / Under the cabbages.

MARLENE. He was always so proper.

JOYCE. Stuck up git, Connolly. Best lawyer money could buy but he couldn't get out of it. She was carrying on with Matthew.

MARLENE. How old's Matthew then?

JOYCE. Twenty-one. / He's got a motorbike.

MARLENE. I think he's about six.

ANGIE. How can he be six? He's six years older than me. / If he was six I'd be nothing, I'd be just born this minute.

JOYCE. You aunty knows that, she's just being silly. She means it's so long since she's been here she's forgotten about Matthew.

ANGIE. You were here for my birthday when I was nine. I had a pink cake. Kit was only five then, she was four, she hadn't started school yet. She could read already when she went to school. You remember my birthday? / You remember me?

MARLENE. Yes, I remember the cake.

ANGIE. You remember me?

MARLENE. Yes, I remember you.

ANGIE. And Mum and Dad was there, and Kit was.

MARLENE. Yes, how is your dad? Where is he tonight? Up the pub?

JOYCE. No, he's not here.

MARLENE. I can see he's not here.

JOYCE. He moved out.

MARLENE. What? When did he? / Just recently?*

ANGIE. Didn't you know that? You don't know much.

JOYCE. *No, it must be three years ago. Don't be rude, Angie.

ANGIE. I'm not, am I, Aunty? What else don't you know?

JOYCE. You was in America or somewhere. You sent a postcard.

ANGIE. I've got that in my room. It's the Grand Canyon. Do you want to see it? Shall I get it? I can get it for you.

MARLENE. Yes, all right. (*ANGIE goes.*)

JOYCE. You could be married with twins for all I know. You must have affairs and break up and I don't need to know about any of that so I don't see what the fuss is about.

MARLENE. What fuss? (*ANGIE comes back with the postcard.*)

ANGIE. "Driving across the states for a new job in L.A. It's a long way but the car goes very fast. It's very hot. Wish you were here. Love from Aunty Marlene."

JOYCE. Did you make a lot of money?

MARLENE. I spent a lot.

ANGIE. I want to go to America. Will you take me?

JOYCE. She's not going to America, she's been to America, stupid.

ANGIE. She might go again, stupid. It's not something you do once. People who go keep going all the time, back and forth on jets. They go on Concorde and Laker and get jat lag. Will you take me?

MARLENE. I'm not planning a trip.

ANGIE. Will you let me know?

JOYCE. Angie, / you're getting silly.

ANGIE. I want to be American.

JOYCE. It's time you were in bed.

ANGIE. No it's not. / I don't have to go to bed at all tonight.

JOYCE. School in the morning.

ANGIE. I'll wake up.

JOYCE. Come on now, you know how you get.

ANGIE. How do I get? / I don't get anyhow.*

JOYCE. Angie. *Are you staying the night?

MARLENE. Yes, if that's all right. / I'll see you in the morning.

ANGIE. You can have my bed. I'll sleep on the sofa.

JOYCE. You will not, you'll sleep in your bed. / Think

ANGIE. Mum.

JOYCE. I can't see through that? I can just see you going to sleep / with us talking.

ANGIE. I would, I would go to sleep, I'd love that.

JOYCE. I'm going to get cross, Angie.

ANGIE. I want to show her something.

JOYCE. Then bed.

ANGIE. It's a secret.

JOYCE. Then I expect it's in your room so off you go. Give us a shout when you're ready for bed and your aunty'll be up and see you.

ANGIE. Will you?

MARLENE. Yes of course. (*ANGIE goes. Silence.*) It's cold tonight.

JOYCE. Will you be all right on the sofa? You can /
have my bed.

MARLENE. The sofa's fine.

JOYCE. Yes the forecast said rain tonight but it's held
off.

MARLENE. I was going to walk down to the estuary
but I've left it a bit late. Is it just the same?

JOYCE. They cut down the hedges a few vears back. Is
that since you were here?

MARLENE. But it's not changed down the end, all the
mud? And the reeds? We used to pick them up when
they were bigger than us. Are there still lapwings?

JOYCE. You get strangers walking there on a Sunday.
I expect they're looking at the mud and the lapwings,
yes.

MARLENE. You could have left.

JOYCE. Who says I wanted to leave?

MARLENE. Stop getting at me then, you're really boring.

JOYCE. How could I have left?

MARLENE. Did you want to?

JOYCE. I said how, / how could I?

MARLENE. If you'd wanted to you'd have done it.

JOYCE. Christ.

MARLENE. Are we getting drunk?

JOYCE. Do you want something to eat?

MARLENE. No, I'm getting drunk.

JOYCE. Funny time to visit, Sunday evening.

MARLENE. I came this morning. I spent the day—

ANGIE. (off) Aunty! Aunty Marlene!

MARLENE. I'd better go.

JOYCE. Go on then.

MARLENE. All right.

ANGIE. (off) Aunty! Can you hear me? I'm ready.

(MARLENE goes. JOYCE goes on sitting, clears up, sits again. MARLENE comes back.)

JOYCE. So what's the secret?
MARLENE. It's a secret.
JOYCE. I know what it is anyway.
MARLENE. I bet you don't. You always said that.
JOYCE. It's her exercise book.
MARLENE. Yes, but you don't know what's in it.
JOYCE. It's some game, some secret society she has with Kit.
MARLENE. You don't know the password. You don't know the code.
JOYCE. You're really in it, aren't you. Can you do the handshake?
MARLENE. She didn't mention a handshake.
JOYCE. I thought they'd have a special handshake. She spends hours writing that but she's useless at school. She copies things out of books about black magic, and politicians out of the paper. It's a bit childish.
MARLENE. I think it's a plot to take over the world.
JOYCE. She's been in the remedial class the last two years.
MARLENE. I came up this morning and spent the day in Ipswich. I went to see mother.
JOYCE. Did she recognize you?
MARLENE. Are you trying to be funny?
JOYCE. No, she does wander.
MARLENE. She wasn't wandering at all, she was very lucid thank you.
JOYCE. You were very lucky then.
MARLENE. Fucking awful life she's had.
JOYCE. Don't tell me.

MARLENE. Fucking waste.

JOYCE. Don't talk to me.

MARLENE. Why shouldn't I talk? Why shouldn't I talk to you? / Isn't she my mother too?

JOYCE. Look, you've left, you've gone away, / we can do without you.

MARLENE. I left home, so what, I left home. People do leave home / it is normal.

JOYCE. We understand that, we can do without you.

MARLENE. We weren't happy. Were you happy?

JOYCE. Don't come back.

MARLENE. So it's just your mother is it, your child, you never wanted me round, / you were jealous

JOYCE. Here we go.

MARLENE. of me because I was the little one and I was clever.

JOYCE. I'm not clever enough for all this psychology / if that's what it is.

MARLENE. Why can't I visit my own family / without

JOYCE. Aah.

MARLENE. all this?

JOYCE. Just don't go on about Mum's life when you haven't been to see her for how many years. / I go

MARLENE. It's up to me.

JOYCE. and see her every week.

MARLENE. Then don't go and see her every week.

JOYCE. Somebody has to.

MARLENE. No they don't. / Why do they?

JOYCE. How would I feel if I didn't go?

MARLENE. A lot better.

JOYCE. I hope you feel better.

MARLENE. It's up to me.

JOYCE. You couldn't get out of here fast enough. (*pause*)

MARLENE. Of course I couldn't get out of here fast enough. What was I going to do? Marry a dairyman who'd come home pissed? / Don't you fucking this

JOYCE. Christ.

MARLENE. fucking that fucking bitch fucking tell me what to fucking do fucking.

JOYCE. I don't know how you could leave your own child.

MARLENE. You were quick enough to take her.

JOYCE. What does that mean?

MARLENE. You were quick enough to take her.

JOYCE. Or what? Have her put in a home? Have some stranger / take her would you rather?

MARLENE. You couldn't have one so you took mine.

JOYCE. I didn't know that then.

MARLENE. Like hell, / married three years.

JOYCE. I didn't know that. Plenty of people / take that long.

MARLENE. Well it turned out lucky for you, didn't it?

JOYCE. Turned out all right for you by the look of you. You'd be getting a few less thousand a year.

MARLENE. Not necessarily.

JOYCE. You'd be stuck here / like you said.

MARLENE. I could have taken her with me.

JOYCE. You didn't want to take her with you. It's no good coming back now, Marlene, / and saying—

MARLENE. I know a managing director who's got two children, she breast feeds in the board room, she pays a hundred pounds a week on domestic help alone and she can afford that because she's an extremely high-powered lady earning a great deal of money.

JOYCE. So what's that got to do with you at the age of seventeen?

MARLENE. Just because you were married and had somewhere to live—

JOYCE. You could have lived at home. / Or live

MARLENE. Don't be stupid.

JOYCE. with me and Frank. / You

MARLENE. You never suggested.

JOYCE. said you weren't keeping it. You shouldn't have had it / if you wasn't

MARLENE. Here we go.

JOYCE. going to keep it. You was the most stupid, / for someone so clever you was the most stupid, get yourself pregnant, not go to the doctor, not tell.

MARLENE. You wanted it, you said you were glad, I remember the day, you said I'm glad you never got rid of it, I'll look after it, you said that down by the river. So what are you saying, sunshine, you don't want her?

JOYCE. Course I'm not saying that.

MARLENE. Because I'll take her, / wake her up and pack now.

JOYCE. You wouldn't know how to begin to look after her.

MARLENE. Don't you want her?

JOYCE. Course I do, she's my child.

MARLENE. Then what are you going on about / why did I have her?

JOYCE. You said I got her off you / when you didn't—

MARLENE. I said you were lucky / the way it—

JOYCE. Have a child now if you want one. You're not old.

MARLENE. I might do.

JOYCE. Good. (*pause*)

MARLENE. I've been on the pill so long / I'm probably sterile.

JOYCE. Listen when Angie was six months I did get pregnant and I lost it because I was so tired looking after your fucking baby / because she cried so

MARLENE. You never told me.

JOYCE. much—yes I did tell you— / and the doctor

MARLENE. Well I forgot.

JOYCE. said if I'd sat down all day with my feet up I'd've kept it / and that's the only chance I ever had because after that—

MARLENE. I've had two abortions, are you interested? Shall I tell you about them? Well I won't, it's boring, it wasn't a problem. I don't like messy talk about blood / and what a bad time we all had. I

JOYCE. If I hadn't had your baby. The doctor said.

MARLENE. don't want a baby. I don't want to talk about gynaecology.

JOYCE. Then stop trying to get Angie off of me.

MARLENE. I come down here after six years. All night you've been saying I don't come often enough. If I don't come for another six years she'll be twenty-one, will that be OK?

JOYCE. That'll be fine, yes, six years would suit me fine. (*pause*)

MARLENE. I was afraid of this. I only came because I thought you wanted . . . I just want . . . (*She cries.*)

JOYCE. Don't grizzle, Marlene, for God's sake.

Marly? Come on, pet. Love you really.

Fucking stop it, will you? (*She goes to MARLENE.*)

MARLENE. No, let me cry. I like it. (*They laugh, MARLENE begins to stop crying.*) I knew I'd cry if I wasn't careful.

JOYCE. Everyone's always crying in this house. Nobody takes any notice.

MARLENE. You've been wonderful looking after Angie.

JOYCE. Don't get carried away.

MARLENE. I can't write letters but I do think of you.

JOYCE. You're getting drunk. I'm going to make some tea.

MARLENE. Love you. (*JOYCE goes to make tea.*)

JOYCE. I can see why you'd want to leave. It's a dump here.

MARLENE. So what's this about you and Frank?

JOYCE. He was always carrying on, wasn't he. And if I wanted to go out in the evening he'd go mad, even if it was nothing, a class, I was going to go to an evening class. So he had this girlfriend, only twenty-two poor cow, and I said go on, off you go, hoppit. I don't think he even likes her.

MARLENE. So what about money?

JOYCE. I've always said I don't want your money.

MARLENE. No, does he send you money?

JOYCE. I've got four different cleaning jobs. Adds up. There's not a lot round here.

MARLENE. Does Angie miss him?

JOYCE. She doesn't say.

MARLENE. Does she see him?

JOYCE. He was never that fond of her to be honest.

MARLENE. He tried to kiss me once. When you were engaged.

JOYCE. Did you fancy him?

MARLENE. No, he looked like a fish.

JOYCE. He was lovely then.

MARLENE. Ugh.

JOYCE. Well I fancied him. For about three years.

MARLENE. Have you got someone else?

JOYCE. There's not a lot round here. Mind you, the minute you're on your own, you'd be amazed how your friends' husbands drop by. I'd sooner do without.

MARLENE. I don't see why you couldn't take my money.

JOYCE. I do, so don't bother about it.

MARLENE. Only got to ask.

JOYCE. So what about you? Good job?

MARLENE. Good for a laugh. / Got back

JOYCE. Good for more than a laugh I should think.

MARLENE. from the US of A a bit wiped out and slotted into this speedy employment agency and still there.

JOYCE. You can always find yourself work then?

MARLENE. That's right.

JOYCE. And men?

MARLENE. Oh there's always men.

JOYCE. No-one special?

MARLENE. There's fellas who like to be seen with a high-flying lady. Shows they've got something really good in their pants. But they can't take the day to day. They're waiting for me to turn into the little woman. Or maybe I'm just horrible of course.

JOYCE. Who needs them.

MARLENE. Who needs them. Well I do. But I need adventures more. So on on into the sunset. I think the eighties are going to be stupendous.

JOYCE. Who for?

MARLENE. For me. / I think I'm going up up up.

JOYCE. Oh for you. Yes, I'm sure they will.

MARLENE. And for the country, come to that. Get the economy back on its feet and whoosh. She's a tough lady, Maggie. I'd give her a job. / She just needs to hang

JOYCE. You voted for them, did you?

MARLENE. in there. This country needs to stop whining. / Monetarism is not

JOYCE. Drink your tea and shut up, pet.

MARLENE. stupid. It takes time, determination. No more slop. / And

JOYCE. Well I think they're filthy bastards.

MARLENE. who's got to drive it on? First woman prime minister. Terrifico. Aces. Right on. / You must admit. Certainly gets my vote.

JOYCE. What good's first woman if it's her? I suppose you'd have liked Hitler if he was a woman. Ms Hitler. Got a lot done, Hitlerina. / Great adventures.

MARLENE. Bosses still walking on the worker's faces? Still dadda's little parrot? Haven't you learned to think for yourself? I believe in the individual. Look at me.

JOYCE. I am looking at you.

MARLENE. Come on, Joyce, we're not going to quarrel over politics.

JOYCE. We are though.

MARLENE. Forget I mentioned it. Not a word about the slimy unions will cross my lips. (*pause*)

JOYCE. You say Mother had a wasted life.

MARLENE. Yes I do. Married to that bastard.

JOYCE. What sort of life did he have? /

MARLENE. Violent life?

JOYCE. Working in the fields like an animal. / Why

MARLENE. Come off it.

JOYCE. wouldn't he want a drink? You want a drink. He couldn't afford whisky.

MARLENE. I don't want to talk about him.

JOYCE. You started, I was talking about her. She had a rotten life because she had nothing. She went hungry.

MARLENE. She was hungry because he drank the

money. / He used to hit her.

JOYCE. It's not all down to him / Their

MARLENE. She didn't hit him.

JOYCE. lives were rubbish. They were treated like rubbish. He's dead and she'll die soon and what sort of life
/ did they have?

MARLENE. I saw him one night. I came down.

JOYCE. Do you think I didn't? / They

MARLENE. I still have dreams.

JOYCE. didn't get to America and drive across it in a
fast car. / Bad nights, they had bad days.

MARLENE. America, America, you're jealous. / I had
to get out, I knew when I

JOYCE. Jealous?

MARLENE. was thirteen, out of their house, out of
them, never let that happen to me, / never let him, make
my own way, out.

JOYCE. Jealous of what you've done, you'd be
ashamed of me if I came to your office, your smart
friends, wouldn't you, I'm ashamed of you, think of
nothing but yourself, you've got on, nothing's changed
for most people, / has it?

MARLENE. I hate the working class / which is what

JOYCE. Yes you do.

MARLENE. you're going to go on about now, it doesn't
exist any more, it means lazy and stupid. / I don't

JOYCE. Come on, now we're getting it.

MARLENE. like the way they talk. I don't like beer guts
and football vomit and saucy tits / and brothers and
sisters—

JOYCE. I spit when I see a Rolls Royce, scratch it with
my ring / Mercedes it was.

MARLENE. Oh very mature—

JOYCE. I hate the cows I work for / and their dirty

dishes with blanquette of fucking veau.

MARLENE. and I will not be pulled down to their level by a flying picket and I won't be sent to Siberia / or a loony bin just because I'm original. And I support

JOYCE. No, you'll be on a yacht, you'll be head of Coca Cola and you wait, the eighties is going to be stupendous all right because we'll get you lot off our backs—

MARLENE. Reagan even if he is a lousy movie star because the reds are swarming up his map and I want to be free in a free world—

JOYCE. What? / What?

MARLENE. I know what I mean / by that—not shut up here.

JOYCE. So don't be round here when it happens because if someone's kicking you I'll just laugh. (*silence*)

MARLENE. I don't mean anything personal. I don't believe in class. Anyone can do anything if they've got what it takes.

JOYCE. And if they haven't?

MARLENE. If they're stupid or lazy or frightened, I'm not going to help them get a job, why should I?

JOYCE. What about Angie?

MARLENE. What about Angie?

JOYCE. She's stupid, lazy and frightened, so what about her?

MARLENE. You run her down too much. She'll be all right.

JOYCE. I don't expect so, no. I expect her children will say what a wasted life she had. If she has children. Because nothing's changed and it won't with them in.

MARLENE. Them, them. / Us and them?

JOYCE. And you're one of them.

MARLENE. And you're us, wonderful us, and Angie's us / and Mum and Dad's us.

JOYCE. Yes, that's right, and you're them.

MARLENE. Come on, Joyce, what a night. You've got what it takes.

JOYCE. I know I have.

MARLENE. I didn't really mean all that.

JOYCE. I did.

MARLENE. But we're friends anyway.

JOYCE. I don't think so, no.

MARLENE. Well it's lovely to be out in the country. I really must make the effort to come more often. I want to go to sleep. I want to go to sleep. (*JOYCE gets blankets for the sofa.*)

JOYCE. Goodnight then. I hope you'll be warm enough.

MARLENE. Goodnight. Joyce—

JOYCE. No, pet. Sorry. (*JOYCE goes. MARLENE sits wrapped in a blanket and has another drink. ANGIE comes in.*)

ANGIE. Mum?

MARLENE. Angie? What's the matter?

ANGIE. Mum?

MARLENE. No, she's gone to bed. It's Aunty Marlene.

ANGIE. Frightening.

MARLENE. Did you have a bad dream? What happened in it? Well you're awake now, aren't you, pet?

ANGIE. Frightening.

End of Play

COSTUME PLOT

Time — one to ten minutes or ten +
Location (Loc.) — off left = O.L.
off right = O.R.
dressing room = D.R.
on stage = O.S.
Indicate pre-set with P.S. after time — also indicate stage location

Isabella/Joyce/Nell:
SCENE 1
Change 1 time —   Loc. — D. Room
+ green stripe pantaloons
+ green stripe midi skirt
+ green stripe jacket w/brn. velvet cuffs and buttons
+ distressed straw hat
+ leather belt w/pouches
+ brown sox
+ brown ankle boots
× underdress — Joyce — worn jeans, purple s.s. knit top
SCENE 3
Change 2 time — 3 min   Loc. — C.R./D.R.
− green stripe pants, jacket, skirt
− hat
− belt w/pouches
− sox and boots
+ gray faded gym shoes
SCENE 4
Change 3 time — 10 min   Loc. — D. Room
− jeans
− top
− gym shoes
+ blk. cotton ankle pants
+ electric blue/brn. silk "zebra" top
+ brn./gold low heel shoes
+ gold clip-on earrings

SCENE 5
Change 4 time — 40 sec.   Loc. — U.L.
- pants
- blue top
- shoes
- earrings
+ worn jeans (same)
+ brown v-neck long-sleeve sweater
+ purple scuff slip-on sweaters

Waitress/Jeanine/Win:
SCENE 1
Change 1 time —   Loc. — D. Room
+ gray fleece swingy miniskirt
+ gray/pink fleece top w/"La Prima Donna" logo — U.R.
+ gray/pink headband
+ 1 gray sock
+ 1 pink sock
+ pink/silver sneakers
× underdress Jeanine nude pantyhose, & white blouse w/lace collar & blue bow
SCENE 2
Change 2 time 40 sec.   Loc. — D.L.
- skirt, top
- 2 sox
- sneakers
- headband
+ pink floral skirt
+ maroon flat shoes
+ navy shoulder bag
SCENE 4
Change 3 time — 10   Loc. D. Room
- skirt

- white blouse
- purse
+ dk. print flower skirt
+ fuschia s.s. t-shirt
+ pink stencil-side heels
+ turquoise/silver belt
+ gray purse
+ maroon frame glasses

Lady Nijo/Mrs. Kidd:
SCENE 1
Change 1 time —   Loc. — D. Room
+ cream satin pants
+ gray w/print kimono
+ peach/orange/gold 7-layer kimono
+ off white tobi sox
+ red wedge sandals
SCENE 4
Change 2 time — 10 +   Loc. — D. Room
- gray kimono
- peach kimono
- satin pants
- sox
- sandals
+ blue stone engage. & wedding ring
+ cream blouse w/large bow
+ blue linen jacket
+ cream/tan/blue plaid linen skirt
+ nude pantyhose
+ tan heels & shoulder bag

Dull Gret/Angie:
SCENE 1
Change 1 Time —   Loc. — D. Room

+ distressed beige blouse
+ distressed red & brn. velvet vest w/2 sleeves
+ gray petticoat
+ brn./gray distress overskirt
+ brn/gray cotton stockings
+ brn. rag shoes
+ armor breastplate
+ blk. leather hat w/attached hair
× underdress Angie: denim skirt, green floral blouse, dirty white knee sox

SCENE 3

Change 2 time — 3 min.   Loc. — D.R. (booth)
− distressed blouse
− 2 skirts
− vest & sleeves
− stockings & shoes
− breastplate
− hat w/hair
+ red scholl sandals

Change 3 time — 1 min.   Loc. — U.L.
− denim skirt
− green blouse
+ "old" blue floral dress

SCENE 4

Change 4 time — 10 +   Loc. — D. Room
− "Old" blue dress
− dirty knee sox
− red scholls
+ denim skirt
+ pink stripe blouse
+ black sandals
+ pink oval drop earrings
+ 2 stripe hair combs
+ multi stone charm bracelet

Change 5 time—40 sec.　　Loc.—c.r.
- pink blouse
- denim skirt
- earrings, combs, bracelet
- black sandals
+ pink w/strawberries t-shirt dress
+ white clogs (distressed)

Change 6 time—2 min　　Loc.—d.r. (booth)
- t-shirt dress
+ "new" blue floral dress
+ multi-color ball & rubber band (hair)

Change 7 time—10+　　Loc.—D. Room
- "new" blue dress
- rubberband
+ blue floral nightgown
- white clogs

Marlene:
SCENE 1
Change 1 time—　　Loc.—D. Room
+ maroon silk tank top
+ lemon satin jacket/slax
+ suntan pantyhose
+ white/gold heeled sandals
+ 2 gold chains
+ gold chain w/horn
+ gold knot earrings

SCENE 2
Change 2 time 40 sec.　　Loc.—c.r.
- satin jacket/slax
- sandals
+ brown silk cowl blouse
+ cream/brown stripe skirt (from suit)

+ heavy long gold chain
+ brown slingbacks
SCENE 3
Change 3 time—10+   Loc.—D. Room
− maroon silk top (replace brn. silk blouse)
+ double breasted suit jacket
+ brown shoulder bag
(leaves jacket & purse on stage)
SCENE 4
Change 4 time—2 min.   Loc.—D.R. (booth)
− brown silk blouse
+ tan brown sleeveless knit sweater
(+ re-dress brn. silk blouse over)
SCENE 5
Change 5 time—40 sec.   Loc.—U.L.
− silk blouse
− suit skirt
− heavy gold chain
− brown sling backs
+ brown linen slacks
+ tan/colored tweed cardigan
+ maroon boots (heels)
+ maroon shoulder bag

Pope Joan/Louise:
SCENE 1
Change 1 time—   Loc.—D. Room
+ white shift
+ cream l.s. gown w/sleeve trim
+ cream chiffon w/lace surplice
+ red velvet hooded cape
+ gold w/red & white stones cross necklace
+ red stone gold ring R-1
+ red felt "Pope" hat

+ white nylon knee sox
+ red flat shoes
SCENE 4
Change 2 time — 10 +   Loc. — D. Room
− shift
− gown
− surplice
− cape
− cross & ring
− hat
− shoes & sox
+ nude support hose
+ teal knit belted dress
+ brown shoes & handbag
+ pearl/gold clip stud earrings

Patient Griselda/Kit/Shona:
SCENE 1
Change 1 time —   Loc. — D. Room
+ cream gown
+ cream hennin w/veil
+ cream low pumps
+ opal ring R-1
× underdress: Kit's white undershirt
SCENE 3
Change 2 time — 3 min.   Loc. — U.L.
− dress
− hat
− shoes & ring
+ red shorts
+ red anklets
+ black sneakers
+ yellow/red stripe + shirt
+ plain white panties

+ white panties w/pouch
+ red plastic barrette
SCENE 4
Change 3 time — 10 +   Loc. — D. Room
− shorts, t-shirt, sox, 2 pr. panties, sneakers,
  barrettes
+ leather pants
+ peach shirt w/stripe bib front (no collar)
+ black/white tweed jacket w/white hankie in front
  pocket
+ black heeled leather boots
+ 2 black hair chop sticks
× underdress: Kit's blue anklets
SCENE 5
Change 4 time — 3 min.   Loc. U.L.
− shirt, jacket, pants, boots, chopsticks
+ red shorts
+ red/white stripe t-shirt
+ black sneakers
+ red plastic barrette

FOOD NOTES

The drinks are all made with burnt sugar.

Soup
Avocado
Waldorf salad
Steaks
Canneloni
Potatoes
Chicken
Side salad
Apple pie & cream
Biscuits
Cheeseboard
Profiteroles
Cake
Zabaglione
Bread rolls
Act 2 yoghurt

Sc 1
Sword
Oval tablecloth
5 menus
Wine list
Waitresses notebook
Dull Gret's basket & sword
Burnt sugar to make drinks
2 brandy bottles
Food — see separate sheet
Potato dish, metal, 2 compartments
5 Frascati bottles
3 baskets
2 flasks to keep gravy & soup hot
3 soup bowls
12 side plates
Paper serviettes
Avocado dish
3 teaspoons
3 pudding bowls
5 dinner plates
Blu tac
Wooden bowl for salad
Basket for cheese biscuits
2 glasses for zabaglione
Cheeseboard & knife with false cheese
Tablecloth (white for on top) — to cover table 8' long
    4' wide
Tray with 6 brandy glasses & linen cloth
Tray with
    6 cups
    6 saucers
    6 teaspoons
    sugar bowl

milk jug
Coffee pot
Glass of water
Cutlery
   6 large forks
   6 small forks
   6 large knives
   6 small knives
   6 dessert spoons
   6 soup spoons
6 linen napkins
6 wine glasses
2 sets salt & pepper
Spare crockery in case they change anything for New
    York run

Sc 2
Perspex clipboards

Sc 3
Dressing for hut—photos, old toys, etc.
Brick
Blood for Kit

Sc 4
Office files & pens
Card index file
Plastic carrier bags + 2 spares
Angies cardigan
Empty yoghurt cartons and tops
Empty milk bottle
Coffee machine with jug of coffee
6 coffee cups
4 white plastic teaspoons
Files dressing (we're sending master copies)

Sc 5
Memphis carrier bag + 1 spare
2 Bells whisky bottles
2 empty teabag boxes
Letter rack
Bills
Blue plastic thing for sink
Oven glove
J cloth
Scourer
4 kitchen tools
Washing up liquid
3 mugs
3 glasses
Fridge dressing:
   Ribena carton
   Fanta & Pepsi cans
   Chunky Chicken can
   2 canneloni boxes
   Safeways bag
   1 litre bottle of lemonade
   Yoghurt cartons
2 blankets
Personal props excluding watches
Box of chocolates all stuck down & packed as new
Box for Angie's dress in tissue paper & wrapped
Caleche perfume in a box & wrapped
Postcard of Grand Canyon
Tray of sand to empty whisky into
3 teaspoons
Glass bowl for sugar
Dirty pan
Tea towel & soap

FURNITURE

Sc 1
  Table (see design)
  6 chairs
Sc 2
  Small coffee table on castors
Sc 3
  Hut frame (see design)
  Ladder for outside
  Big bottle inside

Act 2
Sc 1
  3 desks
  Filing cabinet (on castors)
Sc 2
  Fridge
  Sink
  Table
  2 chairs
  Armchair
  Fabric for office screens or similar.

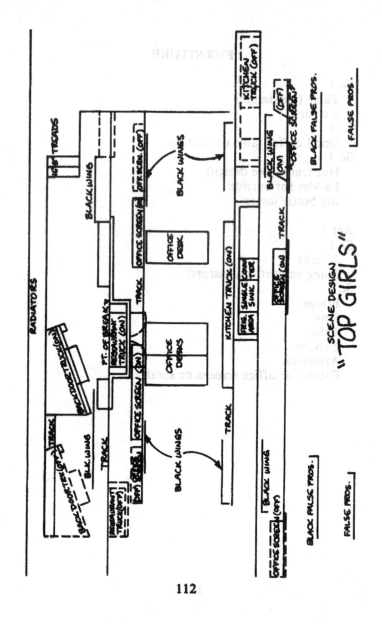

SCENE DESIGN
"TOP GIRLS"